PRAISE FOR *GOING TO WINGS*

"… A palpable and invigorating book, mapping one woman's lifelong efforts to discover her own sexual identity through Christianity and friendship."
--*Kirkus Review*

§

"Sandra Worsham's humor and clear-eyed honesty stitch this amazing quilt of meaning and experience together in a wonderful way."
--Jill McCorkle, author of *Life after Life* and *Going Away Shoes*

§

"The struggle of the gay Christian's complicated effort to reconcile sexuality and faith is often overlooked by church leaders and more secular gays. But it is a complex, and deeply engaging journey. I was deeply moved by Sandra's book, engaged by her voice, her mind, her heart. I think many will find their very human story here in the hands of a wise and compelling woman."
--George Hodgman, author of *Bettyville*

§

"Sandra Worsham is the Mary Karr of Milledgeville, Georgia. This time the *Liars' Club* has extended its boundaries. The personal stakes break the reader's heart as the lies, judgments, and deprivations whirl between Sandra, her family, her friends, her community, and her church. Yet this page-turning memoir of her quest for wholeness isn't mired in despair. Despite the decades that she held her "vile" secret of homosexuality, she kept loving those who thwarted her coming of age. This page-turner oozes with Worsham's grace and grit."
--Amy Lou Jenkins, author *Every Natural Fact: Five Seasons of Open-Air Parenting*

D1205840

"Sandra Worsham loves women and she loves Catholicism. The result of loving both is a dramatic struggle well worth following. Worsham tells her story--one of stunning losses and successes--with admirable style and wit, with charming innocence, and with honesty. I gobbled up this book with delight."

--Bruce Gentry, Professor of English, Georgia College & State University, Editor of the *Flannery O'Connor Review*, and author of *Flannery O'Connor's Religion of the Grotesque.*

§

"'Years later I realized I had committed a murder for I had buried a part of myself.' So says Sandra Worsham in a tender and entertaining memoir about love, family, sexuality, and faith in God. This is a story about growing into life and accepting death, about standing up for yourself while not putting others down, about finding yourself by giving yourself away. I laughed and I cried. I couldn't put this book down."

--Sister Jeannine Gramick, SL, Co-founder of New Ways Ministry, a Catholic organization working for justice and reconciliation of LGBT Catholics with the wider Church, Author of *Building Bridges: Gay and Lesbian Reality and the Catholic Church,* 2006, Laureate of the International Mother Teresa Awards for her role as a human rights activist

§

Other Works by Sandra Worsham

Essential Ingredients: Recipes for Teaching Writing, ASCD, 2001.

Going to Wings: A Memoir, Third Lung Press, 2017

Patterns

PATTERNS
Stories

SANDRA WORSHAM

Illustrations

Letha Hawkins

TLP
Third Lung Press
2018

Publisher: Third Lung Press
Hickory NC

Editing, Layout, Robert Canipe

Cover and Illustrations: Letha Hawkins
Illustrations may not be reproduced without artist consent

www.thirdlungpress.com

"The Traveling Shoe," *Midway Journal*, October, 2015
"The Ola Dress," second place, *Gemini Magazine*, August, 2014
"Pinnacle," 1st in Fiction, Red Hen Press competition, published in *Los Angeles Review*, 2008 ("The Second Mrs. Willis")
"Medusa," *Opium Magazine*, 2007
"The Washer's Husband," *Memphis Magazine*, March, 1987
"Transit," *Carolina Quarterly*, winter, 1986 ("Esther's Real People")
"The Cows Chew Loud in Milledgeville," *Carolina Quarterly*, spring/summer, 1979
"Transients," *Ordinary Time, Winning Poems and Short Stories*, The Church and the Artist Literary Competition, Archdiocese of Seattle
"The Hat," *Ascent*, Vol. 13, No.1, 1987
"The Swimming Hole," *The Chattahoochee Review,* Spring, 1988
"Buster's Night Out," *Western Humanities Review*, Summer, 1980
"Big Productions," *Ascent*, 1985, Volume 10, No. 3 ("Patterns")

"Find beauty, not only in the thing itself, but in the pattern of the shadows, the light and dark which that thing provides."

--Junichiro Tanizaki

For Carmen, Genie, and Judy,
who showed us Grace,
in their living,
and in their dying

For Daddy,
who drew pencil sketches of the writing desk he would build for me,
who painted eyes, nose, and mouth on my imaginary friend

As always,
for Letha,
whose intricate drawings
show us the patterns
in our lives

CONTENT

"The Traveling Shoe"

THE TRAVELING SHOE

"One's destination is never a place, but a new way of seeing things."
---Henry Miller

What will I do when something happens?" asks June. "Something happens" always means death. It is a strange euphemism. It means, "What will I ever do when Maria, the love of my life, is no longer here with me."

I said something similar to my therapist when everything was going well. Teeny was still alive, if confused and moving slowly, and my dog Annie was still alive, if having seizures and wearing a diaper. "I'm afraid something is going to happen," I said in the dimly-lit therapist's office. And what did she do? She laughed. She said, "Well, I can guarantee you that something is going to happen." I wasn't paying her to tell me that. But that was a long time ago, or so it seems now. Now I am with Lauren and, once again, life is good. But not for June. She is in that state of fear that something is going to happen.

We first learn about Maria's cancer when Lauren sees the two of them together at the doctor's office. She comes home and says to me, "Maria is yellow. As yellow as my shirt." Later Betsy and Julia, June and Maria's best friends, come by to tell us the news. "Pancreatic," they say in hushed voices, nodding slowly, looking down. "The death sentence cancer," they say. "This is the worst possible news."

After they leave our house, they are going to make the rounds to the houses of other "family" couples, to tell them the news. That's the way we identify ourselves; we will be there for each other: we are *family*. If we see a couple we don't know, not part of our group, at a concert or at the grocery store, we can *tell*. One of us will punch the other and whisper, "Look, family." On my phone I have set the ring tones to play "We are Family" if any of our friends call.

Being gay is the one thread that runs through us and holds us together. We may not have anything else in common, but we have that—it makes us "other." It puts us on the outside looking in; all of us know that feeling. Lauren and I don't like to watch sports on TV the way the others do. And we don't know how to fix things or use power tools. We also never played softball. We joke that they may not let us join the club. But they do; they are our chosen family, and Maria has the death sentence cancer. Something is sure to happen.

§

June is on her way home from Kroger when she sees the shoe lying beside the road. As she drives, in her mind she is going over how it might be when she gets home. Maria's parents are there from Puerto Rico, and Maria is making Flan. June is supposed to get the Carnation brand evaporated milk, but she hasn't been able to find it and has bought the Kroger brand instead. She pictures how Maria's mother might take the can out of the bag, her brown arm reaching in, the mother with the short gray hair and dumpy body like a pillow with a belt, her skin caramel-colored from the Puerto Rican sun. If the milk is wrong, she will wave her hands in the air and talk in Spanish to Maria about the milk and about June, something that will sound like, "Why can't she ever get anything right? She's like a man, *un hombre*."

When she sees the shoe, June has driven across the bridge beside the power plant, its tall towers shooting into the sky. She doesn't know why she stops, but when she sees the shoe, she puts her foot on the brake, slows down, and pulls into the grass beside the road. Cars continue to whiz past her. The shoe lies there in the tall grass like a dead rabbit and about that long. It is a black-and-white golf shoe, probably the largest size made for a man. It is old and beat up. It looks as if it has been run over by a big truck. She doesn't know what compels her to pick up the shoe and toss it into the back of her truck. She just does.

When she gets home, she is not in trouble about the milk, and for several hours she forgets about the shoe. She doesn't remember it until later, after dinner, when everybody is sitting in the living room watching "Dancing with the Stars."

The next day when she is out watering the flowers in the yard, Maria looks in the back of the truck and sees the shoe. June is down at the end of the driveway getting the mail out of the box when Maria yells after her, "June, what is this shoe in the back of the truck?" June walks down the driveway and when she gets close to Maria, she shrugs and says, "I don't know. I saw it by the road and picked it up."

"Well, get rid if it," Maria says, walking back into the house.

"I'm going to take the garbage to the dump," June says, swinging three large black garbage bags from beside the garage into the truck. She sees the white toe of the shoe sticking out from between two of the bags.

When she gets to the dump and disposes of the bags, the shoe is left in the truck bed. Not knowing why she does it, June picks it up and puts it on the seat beside her. Then she drives to Jill and Susan's house and sticks the shoe into their newspaper box. The game has begun.

§

These are the members of our family. When Lauren and I go to the Brick on Tuesday for "Wings," they are sitting around a long table. "Going to Wings" doesn't mean anything figurative or literary, nothing like freedom or spreading our wings and floating over the sidewalk without shame, nothing about being open about who we are, nothing about the wind beneath our wings. It means that the chicken wings are cheap on Tuesdays. Lauren and I park our car as usual in the lot behind the Tourism and Trade office next to the Exchange Bank. In the fall the three ginkgo trees beside that lot are solid yellow. As we lock the car, I tell Lauren about the short story I wrote in college called "The Ginkgo Tree," about the nursing home where my mother used to work as head nurse and about the symbolism I created between old age and death, and the way the ginkgo tree suddenly drops its yellow leaves almost overnight. That's what will happen to these trees, I tell her. One day the tree will be covered with the yellow leaves, and the next day the limbs will be a bare black skeleton against the blue sky.

When we walk into the Brick, our friends, our family, are circled around the table. Starting from the left are Jill and Susan. Jill has short hair and ran a custodial business before she retired. Susan, blonde and blue-eyed, works in Human Resources for the Piggly Wiggly. Pam, who plays the drums, is sitting beside Susan. Her partner, Linda, lives in Atlanta and works for a computer company. She comes to Milledgeville for the potlucks but not every week for Wings.

Next to Pam are Betsy and Julia who used to work at CDC in Atlanta; when they retired, they moved to Milledgeville to buy a home at Lake Sinclair. June is sitting next to Julia, and Maria is not there because she is having a bad day and is staying at home with her parents. Maria's illness is the reason her parents are visiting from Puerto Rico.

When Lauren and I sit down, Jill is telling everybody about finding the shoe in their mailbox. Julia tells us that Maria's pancreatic tumor is inoperable and that Maria will start chemo soon. Julia takes out a plastic bag from her purse and passes it around the table, giving each of us a purple rubber bracelet that says, "No one fights alone." Everyone but Lauren and me orders wings. Some want mild and all flats; others order medium and all drums; some add celery and bleu cheese dressing. Lauren and I order salads because we don't eat meat.

§

Maria was a nurse before she retired. She is blond and beautiful with a colorful Hispanic personality that draws people to her. People who refer to June and Maria called Maria "the pretty one." Then they follow with, "not that June's not pretty, but you know what I mean." June is tall with short red hair and is the one who cuts the grass and trims the shrubbery but cannot cook and doesn't clean the house. Maria is fanatical about cleaning, washing the towels every day and mopping the floor with wood soap that makes it shine like a mirror. With Maria's parents there, June can't set a half-full coffee cup down without one of them picking it up and washing it. And they all speak Spanish to one another, leaving June out. Maria's mother is constantly patting Maria's cheek and crying, blubbering in Spanish. Maria's father is a handsome silver-haired man with dimples, a dignified Hispanic man who looks wistfully at his daughter and sings "Chiquitita" to her. "Chiquitita tell me what's wrong."

§

June and Maria met in a gay bar in Atlanta. June was on the prowl. She had a reputation for choosing a different woman every month. Maria was supposed to be Miss January. June saw her from a distance dancing a salsa to a pop eighties song, shaking her bootie and stomping her foot, tossing her blonde hair back and laughing, her white teeth and red lipstick flashing in the strobe lights. June went up behind her and put her arms around her. Maria told everyone later that she thought, "What's this old woman doing talking to me?" But Maria became the lasting one. They had a commitment ceremony in Florida at a church, Maria wore a sapphire blue dress with high heels and her hair pulled back with a sparkling barrette. She looked like a Spanish princess. June wore a black tuxedo with a white ruffled shirt. They told us later that June couldn't dance and, during their wedding dance, June was thinking, "Is this song ever going to end?" while Maria was thinking, "Are we ever going to move off of this tile?"

§

Maria is our family nurse. She was a nurse and a nun in a Puerto Rican order. When she realized that the religious life wasn't her calling, she became a nurse who cared for AIDS patients. When the other nurses refused to go into the room, Maria went in and cared for them. This was her calling. When any of us had to go to the hospital for anything, Maria went too. When Lauren had to have a heart catheterization last year, Maria got up at four in the morning to come with us to the hospital.

§

June and Maria's relationship with Maria's parents is better now than it used to be. When they first went to Puerto Rico, Maria's mother told them that they couldn't sleep in the same room, that it was against their Catholic faith. She called June "that woman." Maria told her that "that woman" had a name, her name was June, and if they couldn't have a room together, then they would stay in a hotel and not at their home. The mother then changed her mind. Now, during Maria's illness, they have gained a new respect for June. She is a good caregiver for Maria.

§

Jill and Susan bring the shoe over to mine and Lauren's house when we have the next potluck. They hide it on top of the refrigerator, far back, where it doesn't show. Maria is feeling too bad to come, but June comes and brings Flan, made by Maria and her mother. We don't discover the shoe until I climb up on a step stool to put away the casserole dish I used for my Vidalia onion casserole. Lauren and I talk about creative and funny ways that we can "shoe" the next couple. We decide to mail it to Pam's partner, Linda, in Atlanta. So we do. For a long time we don't hear anything about the shoe.

§

After Maria's parents go back to Puerto Rico, June and Maria take a trip to visit them there. They think it will probably be their last visit. In Puerto Rico, thirty or forty of Maria's relatives gather in the house and pray the rosary. A Spanish priest comes over and says Mass. Maria goes with her father to the church where she was baptized. Her father has promised God that if Maria is able to visit Puerto Rico again, he will walk on his knees to the altar. June e-mails pictures to us of the thin skeletal Maria walking beside her kneeling silver-haired father all the way to the altar.

§

One morning when Betsy and Julia go down to the lake to have their morning coffee, they see something floating beside the dock, a small raft tied to one of the wooden posts by a rope. They walk closer, and there it is, the black-and-white shoe strapped to the dock by a rope, floating and bobbing. "We've been shoed!" they say.

§

When they return to Florida from Puerto Rico, Maria goes to the Mayo Clinic in Jacksonville for a round of chemotherapy. While she is there, Jill and Susan have the potluck at their house. They set up a video camera and we all make a video for Maria. The introductory music is "Ain't no sunshine when she's gone," and the closing is "Lean on Me." Sandwiched between the music are couples, sitting on the sofa in front of the camera, talking to Maria, telling her how much we miss her and that our prayers are with her. Lauren and I sing a duet to her, the Irish Blessing, "May the Road Rise to Meet You."

§

One morning when I am walking in the backyard with the dogs, I see the shoe tied to a tree by the shoestring. I untie it and pull it down, then go into the back door telling Lauren, "Betsy and Julia have shoed us!"

§

We hear that Maria is beginning to feel the effects of the chemo. She is sleeping a lot and has dark circles under her eyes. It is a race between her body and the cancer...who will die first.

§

Tonight I call June and Maria. June tells me that Maria has had a bad day today. She gets chemo again on Monday and then has shooting pains in her stomach on Wednesday. I am thinking of the two of them out there, and they seem so alone to me, dealing with this sickness together. It must be taking everything they have to make it from one day to the next. It has been a long time since they have been together with all of us.

§

June sends an e-mail to everybody, telling us that Maria doesn't have good news. The chemo has not shrunk the viability or the size of the tumor.

§

I pick up Maria and take her to her chemo. Her hair has thinned and is cut short. The blonde has grown out, and her hair is now silver like her mother's. Her eyes look big and brown in her thin face. She tells me that she and June have been talking about which is worse, what Maria is going through or what June is going through. She tells me that, if it were up to her, she would ask the Lord to take her now, but she keeps holding on for June and her family. She says she prays for June every day. She is trying to teach June how to cook and how to wash and stack the towels, that she should put the fresh towels on the bottom of the stack and take the new ones off the top. I don't tell her that Lauren and I repeatedly wash the same ones and hang them back up. She has her way of doing things, and she wants June to learn. She weighs 85 pounds now, but she wears clothes that fit her and dresses up in makeup and earrings. She does not want to look sick, and, despite the way her body is ravaged, she is still a beautiful woman.

§

We've all been talking about death a lot lately. Lauren and I have been writing our own obituaries. We have gone down to my family's plot in Memory Hill Cemetery to see if there will be room for us to be buried there.

§

All my life I have seen symbols. When I was in college at Georgia Southern, each morning when I went to class, I passed a small dogwood tree. For several days the tree held two blooms, side by side. I had been reading *Wuthering Heights* in my English class. One morning as I passed, one of the blooms was gone, leaving a single bloom. I stopped a moment, and, remembering the deceased Catherine tapping on the window of Heathcliff's room in an attempt to be re-united with her love in that space between the living and the dead, I pulled off the single bloom that was left alone on the tree.

§

We are all going to June and Maria's and taking dinner. I will take my sweet potato casserole with the brown sugar and pecan topping; Maria loves it. I will also take my cranberry congealed salad with the nuts and celery and the sour cream topping. Betsy and Julia are bringing several desserts and cornbread dressing. Jill and Susan are bringing green bean casserole. It will be good for us to all be together again.

§

Today when I take my walk beside the lake, I see that the white duck is alone. The geese have left for the winter. Then, waddling from under a bush, is one remaining goose. As I watch, the goose goes into the water, flaps its wings, and then comes back to the shore and waddles up to the duck. The two appear to have become a couple. Geese, I've heard, mate for life. This goose is saying to the duck, I stayed to be with you.

§

Today I notice that my purple bracelet is not on my arm. I panic, afraid that it is a sign. Then I find it on the floor of the closet and put it back around my wrist. I am relieved.

§

Maria is getting worse. She is going through a bout with constipation. The pain medicine causes that. A few hours after eating, she throws up everything. She wants to wear a pain patch so that when she throws up, she won't lose her medicine, but the doctor says she is too light and has no areas of fat on her body to put the patch on. They are going to ask him to put it inside her thigh, where there is a little meat left.

§

Death hangs over our heads, sits on our shoulders. Time goes by. It is summer. The yellow angel trumpet is blooming, the blossoms bowing their heads toward the ground as if praying. One day I come home and find a branch broken, and I think it is a sign. I try to prop the branch up, to make it live, but the next morning the leaves and the blooms have shriveled on that one fallen branch.

§

June says that Maria feels as though a brick is in her stomach. She carries her blue throw-up bucket around with her. June says, "We don't know what else to do." I can tell that caregiving is wearing thin on June, and I tell her to take care of herself, to let someone else take over for a few hours.

§

Lauren and I come up with a clever idea for the shoe. The potluck is to be at Jill and Susan's next time. We go down to the florist's and take the shoe. We ask the woman to plant the shoe in the middle of a flower arrangement, completely camouflaging it with yellow, orange, and purple chrysanthemums and other flowers. Then we have her deliver it to the potluck. It arrives before Lauren and I get there, but everyone tells us that it took them a few minutes to recognize the shoe hidden in the flower. Then it seemed to jump out at them. Everyone agrees that our idea cannot be topped and that it is time for the shoe to be retired.

§

Maria has begun to gain weight, all fluid build-up around her abdomen. The doctor calls the fluid "ascites." The fluid increases every day and has made Maria so heavy that she can't stand up by herself but has to be pushed around in a wheelchair. Finally the fluid seeps from her pores and runs down her legs and puddles on the floor around her feet. June tries taping together Kotex pads to lay across Maria's stomach to collect the fluid. I set up my sewing machine and begin cutting baby diapers into long strips and sewing them together. June tells me that they work much better than the Kotex pads.

§

I go out one evening in the back yard to take the dogs out and find a dead bird lying on the step. Sometimes when that happens, the bird has flown into the window and is stunned. When you pick it up, the bird wakes up and flies away. But this one is dead. It is a purple finch, the bird often described as a sparrow dipped in cranberry juice. Its head and neck are a soft red. Its eyes are closed, and it is beautiful in death. I smooth the soft feathers with my fingers. Its eyes are closed, and its stillness gives me that sad feeling of awe and silence that comes with death. Each death is new, and one never prepares you for the next. I bury the finch in the front flowerbed underneath a small stone angel, my favorite piece of yard art.

The next morning as I make my coffee, I look out the window and see another purple finch exactly like the other one sitting on the rim of the birdbath. It is sitting still and staring, looking stunned. Its feathers are wet and ragged as if it has bathed. It keeps tilting its head to one side. Something in me wants to go and try to wake up the dead bird that I have buried and say, "Come on! Your partner is missing you! You can't go yet!"

Then the finch flies into the weeping cherry tree and perches there among the leaves. Almost immediately several other finches fly into the branches, surrounding the bird.

§

One day June asks me to come stay with Maria in the hospital so that she can run some errands. Maria sleeps the whole time June is gone, and I watch her. All her hair is gone, her head as round and white as an onion, and her chest is hollow. Her fingers on top of the sheet look like bones. Her mouth is open, and her breathing is labored. Her swollen stomach rises under the sheet as if she is pregnant.

When June comes back, she leans over Maria and says, "How are you, Hon?" Instead of looking at June, Maria looks at me and asks, "You'll tell me when it's time, won't you? When it's time for me to let go?"

"You'll know when it's time," I say, "and you'll tell June, and she'll tell you it's okay."

But in truth, it isn't okay with June. It won't ever be okay. June is in denial, is praying for a miracle, which she is sure will come. "You can't go tomorrow," says June. "You're scheduled for an appointment with your doctor."

§

At their next doctor's appointment, the doctor tells Maria and June that there is nothing else to be done, that she can have no more chemo. He recommends Hospice. "But she'll die if we go with Hospice," says June.

§

We take up a collection to pay for the shoe to be put in a shadow box. Betsy and Julia leave it at Maria and June's front door, and it is there when they get home from the hospital. They hang it in the basement, and the shoe is officially retired.

§

Serenity Hospice comes and signs Maria into their program. They bring a hospital bed and a bedside potty chair and many pads to collect the seeping fluids. They give June instructions for Maria's around-the-clock pain medicine. Maria's parents come back from Puerto Rico to stay the duration. Her father is quiet, and her mother cries non-stop and won't leave Maria's side. June never has any time alone with Maria.

§

Lauren wakes me up at 3:00 a.m. She has dreamed that I am cold and dead beside her. We have been talking about death too much. I comfort her and convince her that I am alive.

§

June asks us all to come to their house for Wings. Someone goes to the Brick and brings a big basket of wings, flats and drums and celery with containers of bleu cheese. When we get there, Maria is lying in the hospital bed and is only partially aware that we are there. We are in the kitchen laughing and talking, and the door is open to Maria's room. We take turns going in and out, standing beside her bed, quiet, still, in awe. We lean over and kiss Maria's forehead and whisper that we love her. Her lips move as she tries to whisper back. Someone tells her that the shoe is hanging in the basement in the shadow box.

§

A few days later June calls and tells us that it won't be long. She wants us to come out. We stand around Maria's bed and sing songs, "Amazing Grace," "How Great Thou Art," and a Spanish song that Maria's parents know, something that translates into someone walking beside the seashore and leaving all their belongings in a boat. Remembering that Maria used to tell her dying AIDS patients to follow the light, June turns on the lamp on the dresser. Maria opens her eyes and looks up at all of us standing around her. "I'm ready to go!" she says, her voice momentarily strong, "and you are all holding me back!" When we leave, June is crying. "I knew this would happen if we went with hospice," she says. No one tries to reason with her.

§

That night at four a.m. our phone rings beside the bed. I answer, and June's voice says, "Maria has gone to be with Jesus." She wants us to come out.

I have never driven to Maria's and June's house at night before, and I go past their driveway and have to turn around. When we get there Maria's body is lying there, covered in the sheet up to her chin. Her mother is sitting beside her bed with her hand on Maria's forehead, still warm. June paces back and forth between the kitchen and the death room. The funeral home people are on their way. June has made them promise that they won't put Maria in a black plastic bag. "We don't do that," the man assures her.

While we wait, June and Maria's mother bathe Maria's body. The door is closed, and when they invite us back in, Maria is lying on the bed wearing a red-flowered dress. Powder and lipstick are on her face, and she looks pretty, as if she is about to jump up and put on her dancing shoes.

§

The memorial service is held at Sacred Heart Catholic Church. The priest says that Maria has taught him a lot about what it means to be a Christian and a good person. He looks out at the mourners in the church, most of them gay women, and he says, "Don't let anyone keep you from your faith."

§

One night several days later I dream that Maria has come back. We are all sitting outside around a barbeque, and she comes and sits beside me. I am so happy to see her, and I ask, "What's it like?"

"Heaven is dark," she says, "and there are a lot of old people there."

26

I think in my dream that maybe each person's Heaven is personal, and that maybe Maria's Heaven seems dark to her because we aren't there with her.

§

One day a couple of months after Maria's death, I am driving along the road beside the lake when I see a long black-and-white golf shoe on the side of the road. I can't believe it, and I slam on brakes and pull to the side of the road. I walk back to where the shoe is lying in the grass. I consider surprising someone by starting the game again. Instead, I walk to the edge of the lake and throw the shoe as hard as I can out into the water. I don't know whether it will sink or float, but I like to imagine June, sitting one day on her dock looking out at the lake, when the mate to the traveling shoe washes up on the shore.

"The Swimming Hole"

THE SWIMMING HOLE

"Be not water, taking the tint of all colors."

---Syrian Proverb

Claudia stood in her back yard beside her swimming pool and said aloud, "I don't deserve this." The *this* to which she referred was not the swimming pool which, at that same time last year, caused her to stand there just that way and say, "I can't believe this is mine; it is the answer to a prayer." No, this time what she didn't deserve was the news she had heard on the telephone from her father. When she heard the news, she dropped the receiver on the floor and yelled, "Larry! Come talk to Daddy!" loud enough for her husband working on his jeep to hear.

When Larry heard Claudia's voice, she knew he would drop what he was doing and go inside to talk to her father for her. Then he would come outside and stand beside her at the pool. He would say something practical like, "It isn't going to be that bad" or "Hell, doctors don't know everything." Then he would put his arm around her, and she would cry onto his white cotton tee shirt.

What she had heard her daddy say was, "Dahlia Lee has leukemia." That was when she had thrown the telephone down and run into the yard.

Standing on the side of the pool, she saw her own shadow on the water. Life had been good to her. God had made her pretty. She had large bosoms and a tiny waist. She smoothed her golden hair and tightened the rubber band around her ponytail. She was strong, smart, and talented. She had a wonderful husband. She knew she had everything Dahlia Lee, her twin, had always wanted.

Claudia had told God how grateful she was for all the blessings he had given her. She had told Larry the other day that things had been going right for so long that something was sure to happen. But she meant something less drastic, something like a broken arm.

Dahlia Lee was her twin but didn't look at all like Claudia. Dahlia Lee worked at the auto parts store in Sylvania and still lived at home with their mama and daddy. All her friends were red-neck men who had names like "Spitfire" and "Doodle" and who talked about football and cars. Dahlia Lee had won "Armchair Quarterback" three times and had her picture in the newspaper getting a check for twenty-five dollars for predicting which team would win. The men said she had the best luck of anybody they ever saw. Dahlia Lee said, "Luck, hell! I know my teams!"

Some of the people in Sylvania said Dahlia Lee knew cars better than anybody in Screven County. When Claudia and Larry went back home to visit, somebody was always driving up in the yard and opening up the hood of a truck. Dahlia Lee would go outside and stand for what seemed forever, peering into the motor, pointing and talking. Yet Claudia knew that secretly Dahlia Lee would have given anything to have dates, to have all the things that Claudia herself had.

All of Claudia's life had been enchanted. In the early grades, she was in the high reading group, the Red Birds, while Dahlia Lee sat in the corner with the Brown Birds. On the playground, Claudia pushed the other girls down and yelled, "I'll tell!" when they made fun of Dahlia Lee and called her names. The teachers would say, "Claudia, you and your sister…," as if they couldn't even remember Dahlia Lee's name.

Larry lived down the street then and played with the two of them. When Larry and Claudia pretended to get married, Dahlia Lee was the Preacher. Later when they played Mama and Daddy, Dahlia Lee was their little girl. If they played Doctor, Dahlia Lee was the patient who got the shots and the thermometer in her mouth. And although Larry and Claudia never excluded Dahlia Lee from their games, it was always understood by the three of them that Claudia and Larry would get married someday.

Larry didn't try to hide his feelings. In high school, as Claudia walked down the hall or got on the bus, he was there, the look on his face something Claudia couldn't deny. She wasn't a conquest for him; she was the girl he would love all his life. That was how Larry was; when he made decisions, he made them, once and for all. It had never occurred to Claudia to love anyone else.

Everything Claudia wanted had fallen into place for her, from marrying Larry, to becoming a mermaid at Weeki Wachee Springs in Florida, to owning her own pool and being a swimming teacher. Claudia had always loved to swim and was good at it. She had even saved Dahlia Lee's life one time. They were at a swimming hole in the woods behind their house. They used to climb a tree near the hole, swing from the low branches, and drop into the water. Once after a big rain, Larry had gone with his parents to a family reunion, and Claudia and Dahlia Lee went to the swimming hole alone. Dahlia Lee had climbed the tree and when she swung from the limb, she lost her balance and fell into the water sideways. Claudia saw her sister's head dip under the green water and, wading in up to her waist, had reached out her hand and pulled Dahlia Lee to the bank.

When Claudia and Dahlia Lee were nine, they first saw the mermaids. The family was on a vacation to Silver Springs in Florida when Claudia saw a colorful billboard advertising mermaids down the road, following the arrow. "Let's go see the mermaids!" she had shouted, and their daddy had slowed, swerved, and followed the directions.

At Weeki Wachee, the family went down a narrow stair into an under-water tunnel with a long glass window. Through the glass was the bluest, clearest water they had ever seen. Claudia and Dahlia Lee sat side by side on a bench between Mama and Daddy as beautiful, long-haired girls wearing peacock-blue swim suits with simulated fins and fishtails swam together in circles. One of the mermaids swam close to the glass, took off her goggles, and smiled. Her hair fanned in the water around her head. Breathing air from a snake-like hose that bubbled beside her, the mermaid held her breath and swayed from side to side. When she drank a Coca-Cola and ate a banana, Claudia and Dahlia Lee were mesmerized. Claudia took Dahlia Lee's hand and whispered, "Let's be mermaids when we grow up."

But Claudia saw as they grew that Dahlia Lee wasn't turning out pretty enough to be a mermaid. When they stood side by side and looked at one another in the bathroom mirror and Claudia said, "Let's be movie stars," Dahlia Lee said, "I don't want to be a movie star."

"What do you want to do?" Claudia asked, following her outside.

"I'll think of something," Dahlia Lee said, and began to climb

31

the mimosa tree.

Ever since the day at Weeki Wachee, Claudia talked about her plan. When she and Dahlia Lee went swimming at the community pool, Claudia let herself sink slowly to the bottom of the pool, and felt her hair to see if it was fanning out in the right way. In high school, Larry said, "Honey, you can do anything you want to." And on graduation night, when Larry gave her the diamond he had bought her with his Piggly Wiggly money, she had looked up at him and asked, "Can I still try to be a mermaid?"

"If that's what you want to do, then I want you to do it," he answered.

"It isn't something I'll do forever," she said. "I just want to do it for a while. Will you wait for me?"

"What do you think, you nut," he said. "What else would I do?"

At first Claudia wrote a letter to Weeki Wachee and sent a picture. But she didn't get any response. Then she called. A woman on the telephone told her that they didn't have any openings but that she could apply and be put on a waiting list.

Finally, Claudia asked Larry to take her down there. When they got there, Larry walked around and smoked a cigarette while Claudia sat on a bench with some other girls and waited to be interviewed. When she finally got inside, she talked to a woman behind a desk who told her, again, that they didn't have any openings but would be glad to see her swim.

That was all it took. When the judges saw Claudia in the water, they moved her up to the top of the list. And before she and Larry left that day, Claudia had been hired and was due back with her belongings by the following week.

It took only two weeks for Claudia to learn the thirty-minute show. As she swam underneath the water, the trainer in a sound booth told her what to do.

Her mother asked her on the telephone if she wasn't afraid to breathe through the air hose that waved in the water beside her, if it didn't occur to her that she might suck in water instead. But Claudia said no, she wasn't afraid at all. She loved it as much as she knew she would.

At her first performance, Mama, Daddy, Larry, and Dahlia Lee were lined up inside the glass corridor where she had been with them years before, wishing then that she could be what she had now become. The only imperfection in an otherwise perfect day had been Claudia's wish to make it right for her twin there on the other side of the glass, to make things be for Dahlia Lee the way they had been for her.

A year later when she and Larry got married at their church in Sylvania, Dahlia Lee was Maid of Honor. She wore the lavender ruffled dress Claudia picked for her, and when she complained that she felt like a fool in all that fluff, Claudia laughed and told her she looked prettier than she had ever seen her. "You look like the bride yourself," Claudia said. "You'll take all the attention away from me."

"I hope not," said Dahlia Lee with her poker face. And later at the reception at the house, Dahlia Lee had gone into the back room and come out wearing her blue jeans and a plaid cotton shirt. She didn't even try to catch the bouquet. As they drove off, Claudia heard her say, "I'm better at baseball!" and one of the ushers had said, "You're something else, Dahlia Lee!"

"I hate to leave Dahlia Lee," Claudia said to Larry as they drove down the road. "I hope she's going to be all right."

Claudia and Larry bought a house in Milledgeville where Larry got a job at the sock factory. During the first year of their marriage, Claudia tried to picture herself as a settled housewife who spent all her days making things nice for her husband. But on Sunday, when the Preacher at church talked about the parable of the talents, Claudia started thinking and talked to Larry all the way home about needing a way to feel fulfilled. "There you go," Larry said, putting his arm around her and driving with his left hand. "There you go again—thinking."

Then one day as she was sitting on her back porch working on her suntan, she had an idea. She had been reading *Good Housekeeping* and had fallen asleep with the sun on her face. When she awoke and raised her head, she thought she saw a large pool of water, one that ran all the way to the chain-link fence around the yard. When she shaded her eyes, she saw that she had seen a mirage, that the yard was the same as ever, the same old Bermuda grass stretched out flat and weedy. Between two pine trees hung her clothesline, and on it the yellow-flowered sheets Dahlia Lee had given them for a wedding gift flapped in the breeze.

But right then she knew. That night she fried chicken for supper. Then she told Larry her plan. If they could work out a way to afford a swimming pool, one that would fit into their yard, then she could teach swimming lessons to the children in Milledgeville. And with the money she made, she could pay for the pool herself.

Larry went into the living room and drew figures on a pad. He said he would ask around and see what he could find out. The next night he came home grinning and handed her a picture of a swimming pool, the water in it as blue as that at Weeki Wachee. "How does that suit you, Babe?" he asked.

Claudia didn't sleep much while the pool was being built. All during the night she lay awake and imagined the transformation taking place. First, the large machines rolled slowly through the back woods. Pine trees fell from side to side as a path was cleared. Next, a large red-clay hole big enough to bury a dinosaur in was dug into the back yard. In the woods, a small mountain of red mud rose higher and higher as the displaced dirt was shoveled out by the bulldozer. Next, the iron frames were put into place and the concrete poured. At the end of two weeks, the pool was finished, and Larry had written the first check. The noises stopped, and the yard was quiet again. Claudia sat at the back door of her house and said, "Lord, help me to live up to this."

Then she sat down at the kitchen table with the Milledgeville telephone directory and made a list. She sent letters to doctors, lawyers, and dentists. She looked for the names of people who lived in Walden Woods, the wealthiest section of town. In her letter, she told them she had been a mermaid at Weeki Wachee and had been trained in water safety.

From a catalog Claudia ordered many colored swimsuits with matching sun visors, a different one for each day of the week. Before long, all the weekdays of the summer were filled with lessons.

In the mornings she had the "Moms and Tots" class. Men and women brought their children around to the back yard, all of them walking in flip flops through the grass. Holding their children in their arms, the mothers tiptoed down the steps of the pool and stood waist-deep in the water. Claudia went in with them, and according to her instructions, the mothers patted their children's stomachs, faces, and heads with the water to get them used to it and make them less afraid. At the end of two weeks, the mothers dropped their toddlers off the end of the diving board into the deep water and watched as they floated to the top and paddled to the edge, pulling their faces out of the water and taking their first breath of air.

In the afternoon were the beginners. Claudia stood in the water beside the children and instructed them to hold on to the side of the pool, with their legs out behind them, and to put their faces into the water, blowing bubbles as they kicked their legs.

In the intermediate class which followed, Claudia made each child line up on the side of the pool, and, as she called each by name, the child jumped in the water and swam to her, arms whirling and face up, mouth open, gasping for breath. "Do it again," Claudia said, "and this time keep your face in the water. Be graceful; let go. If you toss around like that, you'll use up all your energy and drown for sure."

During class, the children sometimes said, "Would you swim for us when we get through, Miss Claudia? Would you be a mermaid?" On some days, Claudia went into the house, got her peacock-blue mermaid suit from Weeki Wachee, and, alone in her pool, performed for the children and their parents.

When the family in Sylvania first found out that Claudia and Larry were having a swimming pool built, Dahlia Lee said, "Claudia always has to go overboard about something." But before Claudia knew it, her mama, daddy, and Dahlia Lee started coming sometimes for the weekend. They brought their bathing suits, and Larry grilled hamburgers. Claudia's daddy did flips off the diving board. He and Dahlia Lee splashed water on one another while her mother, standing in the shallow end, held her hands over her face to shield her glasses which were wrapped around the outside of her bathing cap.

When Claudia and Larry went home to Sylvania, instead of sitting and talking with the family, Dahlia Lee kept the football or baseball games turned on the television set all day long, sometimes so loud that nobody could talk. Sitting on the sofa, her straight black hair chopped ear-length all the way around, Dahlia Lee yelled, "Go, Jesus!"

to the television screen, never willing to use the Spanish pronunciation of the ballplayer's name no matter how many times they all told her it was "Hay Sus!" "Don't say 'Jesus.'" Claudia said, and Dahlia Lee said, "Okay, okay." But the next thing they all knew, there she went again, "Go, Jesus! Throw a curve!"

Now standing beside her swimming pool, Claudia felt Larry's arm go around her shoulder. She turned to him and put her cheek against his chest. He patted her hair. "It isn't so bad," he said. "They don't even know if it's the bad kind."

"It is," Claudia said. "I know it is. Things have been too good. I've been standing out here thinking. This makes everything different." Then, looking into Larry's face, Claudia said, "Honey, Dahlia Lee's going to need me. I need to move back there."

"Anything you want, Baby," Larry said. Claudia sat down on the edge of the pool and dangled her legs in the water.

"What about your swimming lessons?" he asked her. "What about the swimming pool? We can't take it with us."

"All I know is that I need to be close where I can be called on," she answered.

For the next several days, Claudia called her students' parents, called home to talk to her mama, packed her suitcase, and read the Bible. She wouldn't look out the window at the swimming pool. Larry went to see the real estate agent, and in two days a "For Sale" sign was up in front of their house. On the weekend, Larry drove to Sylvania to start looking for a job.

When Claudia said her prayers, she told God that if it was his will for her to go through with this, he would give her a sign by letting their house sell and Larry get a job.

She knew in her mind how she wanted it to be. She saw herself and Dahlia Lee arm in arm, going to the post office and the bank and in and out of the hospital getting Dahlia Lee's treatments. She thought they would be like the Haverson sisters who lived in Sylvania and used to go to their church. Emily Haverson was blind and had never been able to look after herself. All her life her sister Louise had been her seeing-eye dog, had held on to Emily's arm and taken her everywhere she needed to go. At church Claudia would see the Haversons sitting several pews in front, Emily's dark hair slicked down close to her head, her ears sticking through, and beside her, Louise in her large-brimmed green hat with the burgundy feather. When church let out, after the benediction, Louise led Emily out to their car, Emily smiling and nodding in the direction of people's voices. The image seemed right and good, so when a couple seemed serious about buying their house, and when Larry got a job in Sylvania driving a truck, she knew that God was answering her prayer.

Claudia and Larry bought a green trailer and put it under the big pecan tree in her mother's and daddy's yard. Claudia told her mother not to tell Dahlia Lee what they had done because she wanted to surprise her. But when Dahlia Lee came home from the hospital, the first thing she said when she saw the trailer was, "I see Claudia's gone off the deep end again." What she acted most pleased about was a large banner across the living room that said, "Welcome home, Sport!" and was signed "Bubba, Lester, Spitfire, and Doodle."

For the first couple of weeks, Claudia stayed over at the house and helped clean up and cook. Dahlia Lee sat on the sofa, watched sports, and yelled at the set. Larry was on the road driving to places like Mississippi, Alabama, and Tennessee. At night, Claudia slept alone in their trailer.

The next week Dahlia Lee got up one morning, put on her blue jeans, and drove herself back to work. When Claudia got over to the house, Mama was sitting at the kitchen table drinking coffee. "You let her go?" Claudia said to her mother.

"Of course," she answered. "When you've been back here long enough, you'll realize that you don't stop Dahlia Lee from doing something she intends to do. You've forgotten."

Claudia began to straighten the living room. "Well, if she collapses up there in the middle of all that sweat and metal and redneck men, I hope you won't blame yourself."

Days went by, and Dahlia Lee acted as if nothing was different. At the supper table, she complained if her mother's pork chops were too tough. Time was when Claudia would have said, "Those who don't do the cooking don't have the right to complain," but not now. Instead, she told herself that one day Dahlia Lee's complaints would be music to her ears. She sat at the supper table looking at Dahlia Lee and thought of how life would be when she wasn't there any more. They all would be saying, "That's how she was," or "I'd give that whole pot of turnips to hear her shout 'Jesus' once." Then they would laugh and say "Dahlia Lee would want us to laugh. That's the way she would want to be remembered."

But Dahlia Lee wouldn't even act as if she knew anything was wrong with her. She went to church only half the time, and the other times she walked in the woods or shot targets. She didn't even listen to the service on the radio when it was broadcast. When the Preacher came to see her, she acted as if she didn't know she was going to die. Claudia would say, "Come in here, Dahlia Lee. The Preacher is going to say a prayer before he goes."

And Dahlia Lee yelled from the other room, "Tell him to go ahead. I can hear him from in here."

When Larry came home on his days off, Claudia said to him, "Dahlia Lee won't even act as if she knows she's sick. I try to do for her, and she acts like she wishes I'd get out from under her feet. Sometimes I think she wishes we hadn't even come."

Each week when Dahlia Lee went back for her check-ups, the doctor said she was holding her own. She wasn't any worse, he said, and she might even be better.

One day while Dahlia Lee was at work, Claudia cleaned up her room for her. That night at supper, Dahlia Lee said, "I'd just as soon folks left my things alone."

"Well, I thought you might like to have a nice, cleaned-up room when you came home," said Claudia.

"Thank you, Sister," said Dahlia Lee, "but if I had wanted my room cleaned up, I'd have cleaned it up."

"She acts like she thinks she can do anything she wants to," Claudia told Larry later, "no matter how it makes other people feel."

One Saturday evening after supper, Dahlia Lee, Claudia, and their mother were sitting on the back porch in rocking chairs watching the sunset. Claudia and her mother were shelling butterbeans. Dahlia

Lee had her feet propped on the railing and was chewing a toothpick. "Think I might go deer hunting with Doodle and them tomorrow," she said.

Claudia stopped rocking and looked at Dahlia Lee. "You've got to be kidding."

"Nope, I ain't," said Dahlia Lee. "Don't see any reason not to. Almost got me one last year. This year might be the year."

"Tomorrow's Sunday," said their mother.

"Good time to be in the middle of nature," said Dahlia Lee. "I can talk to God better out there than I can with that Preacher prancing and snorting."

Claudia sat her butterbeans on the floor beside her chair and stood up. "Dahlia Lee, you're not even trying," she said. "God expects us to do our part."

"Sister, you go ahead and carry on all you want. Me, I got a life to live. I didn't ask you to move down here, and I don't intend to change everything around because you did."

Claudia turned to her mother and said, "Mama, she doesn't even appreciate all I gave up. I gave up everything—my teaching, my swimming pool, everything."

Dahlia Lee said, "Claudia, everything you do, you jump in head first without even thinking. I don't guess it ever one time occurred to you to ask me what I wanted. You don't ask. Then before you know it, you've got in too deep."

The next day Claudia didn't go to church with her mother and daddy. When she got up and went over to the house, still wearing her nightgown, Dahlia Lee had already left. The hunting rifle was down off the rack, and her red-and-black plaid jacket was not hanging on the doorknob.

The house was quiet. Claudia ate a bowl of cornflakes at the kitchen table and then walked around the house. On the table beside the television set was the big white family Bible with the gold-lettered family tree inside.

Off the living room was Dahlia Lee's room. The door was closed, but Claudia turned the knob and went inside. On the wall were Dahlia Lee's banners for her favorite teams. Two pairs of jeans lay across her bed, the knee completely out of one pair. On the floor of Dahlia Lee's closet were three pairs of heavy shoes like men's shoes and not even one pair of high heels, not one pair of anything that looked like ladies' shoes. On the hanging rack in the closet was not one dress, not one skirt.

Claudia walked over to the closet and picked up a pair of heavy brown oxfords. Taking off her pink bedroom slippers, she slipped on the shoes, first one and then the other. They still wore the same size, but when Claudia walked across the room, Dahlia Lee's heavy shoes felt bigger.

On Dahlia Lee's dressing table was a picture of Claudia and Dahlia Lee when they were children. She picked up the picture and studied it, covering first their eyes and then their lips to see which of their features were alike. Claudia's lips were full and round; Dahlia Lee's, thin. Dahlia Lee had almost no chin, and her ears stuck out through her hair. Claudia had her arm around Dahlia Lee's shoulders. Dahlia Lee stared solemnly straight ahead toward the camera. Claudia sat down. The tortoise-shell brush on the table was full of Dahlia Lee's dark hair.

Resting on her elbows on Dahlia Lee's dresser, Claudia cupped her face in her hands. "What's happening?" she said into the mirror. "Nothing's working out."

Then, walking across the room and looking out the window toward the woods where Dahlia Lee was hunting, Claudia said, "I'd be so scared. If I was going to die, I wouldn't be able to think about anything else. I don't know why she's not scared."

In her gown and still wearing Dahlia Lee's shoes, Claudia walked out of the house and into the grass. Stretched across the yard were four sets of white sheets hanging on the line. Parting a top sheet and a fitted sheet, Claudia stepped between them as though stepping onto a stage. Close to the edge of the woods was the old swing set she and Dahlia Lee used to play on as they hung like monkeys from the bars and swung so high that the poles pulled out of the ground. It was so rusty now that it wasn't good for anything.

Calling Dahlia Lee's name, Claudia stepped into the woods. The swimming hole couldn't be far. When they were children, Dahlia

Lee had followed Claudia into these woods, Claudia beating down the leaves and pushing the sticker bushes out of Dahlia Lee's way. Dahlia Lee had followed behind her so close that if Claudia stopped and said, "Quiet! I hear something!" Dahlia Lee bumped into her from behind.

The swimming hole was dried up and covered with leaves and straw. Claudia stepped into it and looked around. To her left was a triangle of pine trees where she and Larry and Dahlia Lee had played house. She reached up and broke a loose limb that hung low over her head. Once flexible, it was now stiff and brittle.

"Dahlia Lee! Dahlia Lee!" she called. Suddenly Claudia heard a loud noise, a gunshot. She covered her ears and fell to her knees.

"Hey!" she yelled. "I'm in here!" She crouched, curled in the straw and leaves, and listened. After a few moments she heard something coming through the brush.

"Jesus God, what are you doing, Sister!" yelled Dahlia Lee as she emerged from the woods, her rifle in her hand. "Hold it, boys!" she yelled. "Hold it! Don't shoot! It's Sister!"

Dahlia Lee ran to Claudia and threw herself down beside her. "Don't you have any sense?" she said, putting her hands on Claudia's shoulders and shaking her. "What are you doing here? I thought you were a deer! Oh, God in Heaven, I thought I'd got him!"

Claudia looked up at Dahlia Lee and threw her arms around her neck. Sobbing, she said again and again, "I'm so scared. Please, Dahlia Lee, don't leave me."

Dahlia Lee laid her gun on the ground and knelt beside Claudia. And for that moment, while Larry drove his truck toward home, while the Preacher at church said his final amen, while the hunters put their guns away for the day, the two sisters consoled one another that the inevitable might be postponed.

"The Second Mrs Willis"

THE SECOND MRS. WILLIS

"We are closest to God in the darkness, stumbling along blindly."

Madeleine L'Engle

I married my English teacher because he got me pregnant. Then he got fired from his job, and now we have nothing. All day he sits on the sofa with his feet stretched out in front of him, makes plans, and tries to forget the past. I sit across from him, roll my Salem 100's package into a ball, and watch to be sure he doesn't call up anybody. When I go to the bathroom, I drag the telephone with me so that I can be the first to answer if it rings.

Mr. Willis tells me that sometimes I act as crazy as his first wife, whom he divorced in order to marry me. When he says things like that, it hurts my feelings, and I go get in his red Horizon and drive around a while, leaving him there alone with Alice, who is one-month-old today. I go into town to the post office and call to see if the line is busy.

Mr. Willis says he married me because we had been through so much together. I think he married me because I'm the only one who ever figured him out. I'm only sixteen, and he's thirty, but if you look at what I've been through, I'm old enough to be his mother.

The Preacher is not my daddy, but he has been my mother's husband since before I was born. One day when my mother was working at the restaurant and I had been in her womb for six months, she looked up from where she was spooning mashed potatoes in big round mounds at the buffet and saw out the window a man leaning a large piece of board up against the front of the restaurant. She was wearing her black-and-white uniform, and she rinsed off her hands and dried them on the apron with the white ruffled trim and took a few steps toward the front window. That was when the Preacher came through the door and saw her standing there pregnant, saying, "What in the world is that?"

"My cross," the man said. "Hope you don't mind if I prop it up against your place here long enough to have me some lunch and be on my way."

"It sure is a big one," my mama said. "Probably bigger than the real one."

But when he sat down at her table and she stood over him, resting her notepad on her belly, writing his wishes in a list right down to the banana pudding for dessert, he decided to stay longer.

After the lunch hour, he called over to her, "Why don't you join me for a while before I move on?" Mama took off her apron, fixed two cups of coffee, and brought them to his table.

Mama has always been an accepting sort of person; where most people would have stayed away from the Preacher with his cross, Mama took it that the cross came with him. To her, the Preacher came up on his cross the same as a teenager on his motorcycle or the mayor in his LTD. That is one reason she is such a good waitress, because what you see on her face is exactly what you get.

That afternoon she leaned her face on her hand, stirred her coffee, and looked at the man across from her who had come into town on a cross. He had dark auburn hair, parted down the middle and slicked flat with Vitalis. His nose and mouth were large and round. He had on a brown suit that looked as if he had been to a wedding or a funeral out of town and had to ride a long way in the back seat coming home. He had sad gray eyes which looked harmless enough, and so when he asked her, Mama told him that my real daddy had made all sorts of promises which he never intended to keep and that she was the type who could never give up her baby, with or without a husband.

When he looked at the woman across from him, the Preacher saw a young Magdalene. She leaned her cheek against her hand, and her brown hair flipped up at her shoulders. She had believed what a man told her, and she would again. The next man who came to convince her might be a scoundrel too. This young woman would never learn not to trust.

When my mama asked about his cross, the Preacher told her everything he knew. Once, when he was young, he had stolen some money from a gas station and found himself in a boys' training school. He made friends there that he shouldn't have made. One night his friends convinced him to come with them, over the high fence and

44

down the road to a man's house where there was a truck and a way out of town. That night, somebody shot an old man as he stood at his back door. The Preacher had stood and watched, and when the man fell, he had run away. As he ran, he had heard the voice of a girl call out, "Granddaddy!" He had been in prison for fifteen years. He wanted to start a Mission when he found the right place to park his cross.

Late in the afternoon when it was time to lower the blinds to keep the afternoon sun from coming in the windows too brightly, Mama and the Preacher were still there, sitting at the table drinking coffee. The sun hit the wood of the cross and made a long straight shadow across the floor of the restaurant.

Mr. Willis' first wife was named Janice. Sometimes when we sit here together on the sofa, I think I can picture how she must have looked over there in the big blue-flowered armchair, asleep, her head dropped to one side. Mr. Willis says she went to sleep all the time, even when they had company. He says that sometimes he had a hard time waking her up, even to come to bed.

Mama had the Preacher over for supper that night, and he never left. He married them himself, the two of them standing side by side in front of the full-length mirror in the hallway, him saying the minister's part and the words of the groom as well. "And now I pronounce us husband and wife," he said. Then, using the tripod and the timed-release camera, he made a wedding picture of them, snapping the shutter and running to stand beside Mama, smiling just in time.

When I was little, after hearing the story many times, I stood looking up at that picture on the wall and thought of how pretty my mama looked on her wedding day. Often stopping in front of the mirror in the hall, I crossed my hands at my waist and said, "I do," and "I do." The Preacher slid his cross under the trailer longways where it lay stretched out straight and cool in the dark sand like some old hound dog, tired after hunting. Later when sometimes he took it out, the crossbars bumped the bottom of the trailer, and vibrations moved under the floor like small earthquakes.

By the time I was five, the Preacher had his Mission established there at the trailer. The sign out front read, "Come unto Me, All Ye Who are Heavy Burdened." At all hours of the night the blue and gold lights beamed across the yard and into my window. When the doorbell rang, I pulled myself up to the window to see the dark figures under the yellow light over the front door. The Preacher padded down the hall in his slippers, his brown plaid flannel robe flapping behind him.

On those nights I climbed out of my bed and went across the hall to Mama to snuggle into the Preacher's warm place. As I fell asleep again, I heard the soft voices of the heavily burdened, asking, pleading, and sometimes sobbing. They all called him Preacher. So did Mama. So did I.

When I first got in Mr. Willis' class, all I wanted was to hurry up and finish school so that I could get out on my own. The Preacher was getting on my nerves, and Mama never said anything to him. So when Mr. Willis told the class he wanted us to buy a journal and write three pages a day of whatever was on our minds, I started writing a little at a time until I had told him everything.

The Preacher's Mission got written up in the newspaper. A pimply-faced young reporter came out and walked around the room making notes of everything: the picture of Jesus in the Garden hanging on the wall over the television set, the table in the corner with the open Bible and the candles, the guest book beside the door. The Preacher refused to let the man from the newspaper copy down any of the names. The reporter was nervous and looked down at me like he wasn't sure what to talk to children about. He made the three of us line up on the sofa, and he snapped a picture. Then he asked the Preacher if he would consider posing beside the sign out front with his cross. That was when the Preacher told the boy he had written enough and showed him the door.

Soon after that, the Preacher got his own radio program, a fifteen-minute spot introduced by the hymn "What a Friend We Have in Jesus" sung by the Johnson Family Quartet.

When I was six, Mama and the Preacher decided that I ought to be a member of an organized church so that I could be around children my own age. So she took me down to Spring Hill Baptist where she herself was baptized when she was a girl, and I became a Sunbeam.

Mama left me at the side door to the church with a woman who had a body like sofa pillows. The woman took my hand in her big warm one and led me inside to sit me down in a small wooden chair beside six other girls. She put our chairs into a horseshoe and pulled a larger one for herself to make a circle. Then she told us about Jesus and taught us to call ourselves Sunbeams.

The first time I saw Mr. Willis in the tenth grade at Milledgeville High School, I didn't think he was cute. His hair is cut short now, but then it was long, and his glasses made him look like a bookworm. If you saw him and you didn't know him, you wouldn't think there was anything special about him. He would look like anybody else. If he stood at your door to sell you some encyclopedias, you wouldn't have any trouble telling him no and sending him on his way.

It was his personality that made him different. I think it will be hard to explain because you have to know him. But it was like this: every day was different. If I was late to class and was walking down the hall, I could hear the class already laughing, and I would walk faster for fear I would miss something. When I walked in, he winked at me, and his grin was so big it made me smile back. I think all the girls were in love with him.

After Sunbeams came Girls' Auxiliary, G.A.'s. When I moved up to G.A.'s, it was like a promotion. In Sunbeams we sang and clapped and sat in a circle listening to stories. G.A.'s meant responsibility.

The first day Mama carried me to G.A.'s and let me out, I looked back at her car as it drove through the cemetery and around the corner; then I looked ahead to the basement floor where I could not go, where all the girls met who were younger than I. As I climbed the stairs to the second floor, I looked up to the gray door at the top and thought that it looked like a door too heavy for me to push by myself. But when I got there, in the room sat all the same Sunbeams who had been down below.

The two counselors, Mrs. Martin and Mrs. Pierce, gave us books called "Forward Steps." These books were to show us how we could move up and what rewards we would receive when we got there.

The choices were:

(1)   Maiden: to receive a green octagon to be worn on the heart.

(2)   Lady-in-Waiting: to receive a white star to be worn in the center of the green octagon worn on the heart.

(3)   Queen: to receive a gold G.A. emblem to be centered on the white star. Also to be crowned with a gold cardboard crown.

(4)   Queen-with-a-Scepter: to receive a gold Scepter with green-and-white streamers.

(5)   Queen Regent: to receive a green satin cape.

In order to receive the reward, we had to do the following:
Memorize scripture.

Learn the names of the Baptist Missionaries in the foreign countries and pray for them on their birthdays.

Embroider a large map of Paul's Missionary journeys.

Visit the shut-ins.

And more.

The awards were presented by Mrs. Martin and Mrs. Pierce at a special ceremony called a Coronation, held once a year in the church sanctuary. All year we spent preparing, trying to meet the deadline. On that night, each girl stood before the congregation and recited one of the scripture passages she had learned. Then she received her reward and her title.

It was after I became a G.A. that the Preacher first started messing with me. When I got home from school, Mama was still down at the restaurant. I put my books down and then looked up at the Preacher, who was sitting in the chair beside the television set with his Bible open on his lap. He watched me fix myself a snack and then started in on me. "Look at me," he said. "Look. You got to be aware every minute. Read the Bible. Pray. Be prepared for the change to come."

Sometimes the way he looked at me made me feel scared, and I went to the front yard and climbed up in the mimosa tree. I sat among the fan-shaped leaves and peach-smelling blossoms and looked down at the yard and the street. In the mimosa tree was a crevice where the ants marched to and fro, often carrying large bundles in their jaws. Leaning close, I watched and felt like God looking down and observing his people busy living their daily lives, never appearing to think of anything important as they traipsed back and forth. Yet I knew, had learned in school, that ants lived to preserve their queen, that all their bundles, all the miles and miles of walking and toting up and down tall blades of grass, all the sniffing and lugging, all the climbing through moon-surfaced sides of tree trunks, were for her, the one they protected more than themselves, the one who held their colony together, who gave them a common reason for existence, who kept them from squabbling among themselves.

Sometimes as I sat high and watched, the Preacher came out and dragged his cross from under the trailer. He stopped under the tree, looked up at me, and told me not to fall and to get my lessons. As I watched him drag his cross down the street toward town where Mama was at the restaurant, he got smaller and smaller. In the distance, he looked as small as an ant.

I was nine when I was baptized in the cement pool down the hill from the church along with six other girls from my Sunday School class. Wearing white cotton robes with only a slip underneath, we stepped into the pool one step at the time, the cold spring water coming higher and higher over our ankles, past our knees, to our waist. The white cotton billowed around us like pillows on the surface of the water. The Preacher and Mama stood on the bank with the other parents. The Preacher was dressed up in a suit. He stood solemnly as each of us emerged from the water spitting and spluttering.

"Dear Mr. Willis and Journal, Here I am writing down the things that happen to me. My step-daddy is getting on my nerves. When my Mama is not at home, he comes in my room and puts his hands on me. First he acts nice, hugging me like a daddy; then he backs off and calls me names of things that I'm not. I am not any of those names he calls me. Today my neck is sore where he pulled it. I want to think of somewhere to go after school before Mama gets home."

For two weeks every summer, the girls in Girls' Auxiliary go off to summer camp at a special G.A. camp in the mountains of north Georgia. The camp is called Camp Pinnacle because it is located on the top of a mountain by the same time. The first time I went, I was ten years old and working on my Maiden Forward Step.

It was the first time I had ever gone off and stayed in a place with other girls. I remember them, clustered around me like soft padding—up the narrow dirt pathway in the woods leading to the clearing for vespers, in the cafeteria clinking silverware, in the chapel singing as the piano played, "Just as I am without one plea," at night in our narrow cots, the soft breathing around me like whispers.

All day we spent in separate rooms of a large building learning our Steps and telling one of the Counselors when we were ready to recite. The Counselor sat beside us and prodded when we forgot. Then she penciled in a check and her initial into our book. I recited about a Legion of Demons who, when they left a man because of Jesus, went into a herd of pigs, and the herd charged down the bluff and were drowned in the lake.

In the evenings when the sun had gone behind the trees and the sky was blue-gray, we walked in a line to the prayer spot in the woods where we sat on sagging wooden benches, which were rough and splintered, and we had sentence prayers. It was so quiet in that place that it seemed to me that God had to be there all around. I imagined him in different forms. Sometimes I thought he was like the Green Giant standing over the circle of trees, friendly but large enough to be threatening. At other times it seemed that he had no shape at all but was in the particles in the air, in the sound of a girl's voice. At these times, the prayers seemed real, and I was sure they were heard, completely absorbed by the spirit of the air, into the trunks of the trees, the birds singing high in the air, the fabric of our clothing, and the shoulders and arms of those girls sitting near me.

One night after the lights had been turned out, a group of the girls in my cabin gathered together on several of the beds and began whispering in the dark. I sat up, and in the light of the moon coming through the window, I saw a large girl named Shannon Avery propped on her knees, her hands motioning to the other girls, and whispering to them. The moonlight lit the corner of her cheek in a ghostly white splotch, and her jaw moved up and down as she exaggerated her words in order to make the others understand.

Quietly I turned my sheet back and crawled on my hands and knees across the beds until I neared the edge of the group. Then I sat straight, hugged my knees to my chest, and listened, my eyes wide in the darkness.

"Where were your parents?" one of the girls asked Shannon.

"They weren't home yet," the large girl answered. "They don't ever get home until after six. I knew they wouldn't be there. That's why I told him he could come then."

"What if you get pregnant?" asked another.

"Oh, I won't," answered Shannon. "We used protection."

As I listened and stared at the group of girls, I was filled with a strong feeling of something like sadness and guilt, all rolled up together. When I lay back down in my bed, I wanted to go home. I wanted to crawl into bed beside my mother.

The side of the mountain behind the woods where we had vespers slanted downward like steep steps. It was to the side of this mountain that we went every morning early for meditation. We took our Bibles and held to limbs and trunks as we eased our way down to a spot beside a tree or a big rock and then into a sitting position where we could listen to the morning sounds and wait for God to speak to us through the Scriptures. The Counselors told us to be careful and not to go far down the mountain. As I read the Bible and tried to feel the presence of God, it seemed that I could see the tumble of my dress, my sweater, and my shoes and socks down the mountain rolling over and over as I saw myself lose balance. It seemed that I could scream all the way to the bottom, far into the green valley at the foot of Mount Pinnacle.

When the mimosa died, I conquered the pecan tree in the backyard. It was an entirely different experience. Where the mimosa tree was smooth, and I could put my cheek against its cool surface, the pecan bark was rough and unpleasant to my skin. Instead of smelling like peaches, the pecan leaves smelled hot, like pepper. Where the mimosa limbs spread broad and close to the ground, the pecan tree shot straight into the air, its limbs far apart from one another. There were no neat crevices in which to sit. I had to cling high in the air, and beneath me, the next limb was a full leg-length away. Where the mimosa limbs had been flexible and easy to ride to the ground, the pecan limbs stood out crisp and brittle, more easily broken than bent.

When Mr. Willis gave me my journal back, I was surprised at how much he had written. In the margins in navy-blue ink were his tiny scribblings that I traced again and again with my pen, trying to make out each letter. "Life is hard, life is hard...," he had written. And, "I know; oh, how I know..." It seemed to me that behind the need in his voice he was saying to me that, however hard my life had been, his had been harder. Feeling older than he was, I began to watch him for signs.

Every day at lunch the girls in the class gathered around Mr. Willis' desk and flirted with him. Sometimes I stood leaning against the lockers outside his door and ate my sandwich there.

I wrote in my journal all the time, in my other classes and in my room at night. When the Preacher came and stood in my door, I hid my journal behind my other books so that he would not become suspicious and wish to pry.

"Dear Mr. Willis and Journal, In fourth grade my teacher worried that my clothes were as neat at the end of the day as they were at the beginning. She wondered if at recess I didn't play. One day she followed me to the playground to the tree I sat beneath. Sitting down beside me, she asked, 'Don't you ever play softball?' 'I thought softball was a boy's game,' I told her. 'Girls can play too,' she told me, and she made me stand so that we could toss the ball back and forth between us. Soon, the spot was filled with the boys from my class, crowding in, intercepting the ball, running and pushing, the day spoiled."

Mr. Willis wrote in my journal that his mother never let him play at all, that he went to his first baseball game only after he was grown. Now he is twenty-six and is no longer a member of his mother's religion, which never let him play.

One day when I got home, a family was at the Mission, a mother and a father and a teenage girl. The girl sat on the sofa between her parents. She had stringy hair that fell across her face when she lowered her head for the Preacher's prayer. Her old-fashioned dress hung almost to her ankles. She sat with her hands folded in her lap and her feet close together, and I noticed that she wore white fold-down socks, the kind I used to wear when I was young.

After they left, the Preacher came into the kitchen where I was putting some ice into a glass for a Coke. He grabbed my arms, pointed out the door at the people getting into their car, and said, "Now, there goes a good Christian girl. You could learn a lot from her."

"Why isn't she in school today?" I asked, and the Preacher knocked the ice tray out of my hand onto the floor.

Mr. Willis sits across from me now writing in a notepad. I can't tell what he is writing. Alice is growing up. Her body, lying on the quilt, covers five whole squares. As I watch the two of them, I am thinking of something I heard the Preacher say. A young couple had come to the Mission. The young woman held a dead baby wrapped in a blanket. The baby had died in the middle of the night from crib death. The Preacher was not able to bring it back to life as they had hoped. Instead, he said to them, "There is one thing in all of us that can never be killed. We can move it from one place to another. We can change its focus. We can look hard at it and beat it on its head and shoulders. We can pierce its heart with a knife. We can caress and talk nice to it. We can love it or hate it. But we can never kill it, no matter how hard we try."

I wrote this once in my journal to Mr. Willis. He wrote back in the margin, "Interesting…" which is what teachers write when they don't know what else to say.

Where we are now is in the house where Mr. Willis lived with his first wife during the time they were married and I was in his class. I imagine her soft feet padding across the floor.

I saw her only once when Mr. Willis asked me over. He wanted me to see a movie called "Apocalypse Now" which was supposed to be like the book we were reading, *Heart of Darkness*.

When I rang the doorbell, Mr. Willis answered, smiling and friendly the way he was. Mrs. Willis was a blonde woman who looked thin and tired. She wore a loose cotton dress. She sat beside Mr. Willis on the sofa and folded her arms. Her elbows were thin pointed bones, her arms like skeleton arms. As I watched the movie, out of the corner of my eye, I could see her white moon face turn full toward me, back half to Mr. Willis, back full toward me. After twenty minutes, she was asleep, her head resting on Mr. Willis' shoulder, her breathing soft in and out. Mr. Willis looked over her head at me and winked.

In class sometimes I looked up and caught Mr. Willis watching me. One day he handed me a folded note that said, "Would you like to go for a ride after school today?"

I thought of the Preacher at home, looked up, and nodded. After class as I passed him in the doorway, he whispered, "Meet me here after sixth period."

Before I could get into his car, he had to clean out the floorboard and the seat, tossing tapes into the back, their plastic cases clattering against one another. On the back seat were probably as many as twenty-five books stacked in piles of five or six each.

"Were you surprised when I asked you?" he asked as he pulled into the highway beside the school.

"I guess," I said. "Why did you?"

Smiling, he looked back and forth from me to the road. He drove fast toward the country. He shrugged. "My students are my friends," he said. "I guess my friends are the most important thing in the world to me."

I didn't know what to say, so I sat and watched out the window at girls and boys who had gotten off the school bus and were on their way home up a dirt road. They flashed by in shades of blues and reds, their arms waving, their book bags slinging into the air.

"Your quietness intrigues me," he said. "You aren't silly like the other girls."

At a Quickie store, he bought two Cokes. Then he reached into the glove compartment over my knees, took out a small picture, and put it in my hand. "That's me," he said, "when I was in high school." His hair was lighter than it is now, and he wasn't wearing glasses. His thin face looked like a boy's face.

The first time I called him, I dragged the phone into my room and closed the door. When Mr. Willis answered, he sounded glad it was me. "Can you talk to me?" I asked.

"Of course," he said. Our conversation was about the books we were reading in his class, about the country music songs he sometimes wrote, and about our childhoods. I could hear the television in the background. I kept thinking he would say he had to hang up, but it was the Preacher who opened my door first and gave me a look, pointing at his watch.

Every day Mr. Willis and I watched for each other. "Come to school early tomorrow," he said. "I'm always here early, and we can talk in my room." I told Mama and the Preacher that I was getting extra help with chemistry, so Mama would take me in on her way to the restaurant. Some mornings I got there before Mr. Willis and was leaning against his locked door with my books in my arms when the other teachers started coming in, one by one. They looked at me as they unlocked their doors. Students weren't supposed to come into the building until ten after eight.

When Mr. Willis bounced down the hall carrying a big box of our journals in his arms, his hair flopping up and down on his head, sometimes the other teachers came out of their rooms and looked at him. He unlocked the door, put the box down on the corner of his desk, put his big hand on the top of my head, and said, "Hey, Girl."
One day he asked me again to ride around after school. I said I would, and as we left, I noticed some of the other teachers looking at us and talking to one another.

This time, instead of driving toward the country, he drove in the other direction to a spot down a dirt road and along a pathway into some woods. He parked his car in a clearing. "This is pretty, isn't it?" he said. "This is one of my favorite places." Pine trees and sweet gums made a circle around the spot, and in the woods the brown needles and big leaves lay together in a thick layer like a quilt.

He got out, came around and opened my door, and took my hand. He led me over to sit in a green spot next to a tree. "Look," he said, still holding my hand and pointing up to the round triangle of sky above us. Then he put my head against his chest, stroked my hair, and said, "Little old sweet thing, little old girl." I closed my eyes, and his voice and his hands and his sweater against my cheek made the world as close to heaven as I ever wanted to get, and the Preacher and all his high-falluting ways were as far away as if they had never happened.

Then Mr. Willis put his hand under my chin, turned my face up to his, and said, "Little old sweet freckled plain thing. You tear my heart out, you know that?" And then he kissed me on the mouth, and his mouth was soft and wet and surrounded me with sweetness. Walking back to the car, we threw large handfuls of leaves at one another.

"Life isn't all serious," he told me, but when he leaned in my car window and kissed me again, I knew that it was serious enough. That night I lay in my bed wide awake. The Preacher was snoring in the next room. I lay on my back, looked out the window into the sky, and touched myself, pretending my hands were Mr. Willis' hands.

The next day I couldn't look at him or talk. It was unbearable to sit in his classroom and watch him walk up and down and smile at the other students and hand their journals back to them.

That day at lunch he told all the others to leave, that he needed to grade papers. He moved two desks into the corner near the window where we couldn't be seen by students and teachers passing by. There with a literature book open between us, our hands under the desktop, our knees touching, for the first time I was glad the Preacher had made me wear a skirt. Mr. Willis slipped his hand farther and farther along the inside of my leg and looked into my eyes until I thought I would die with the secretness.

It was like I didn't even know what I wanted, like something I was born with and had always known about and had probably learned when I was in my mother's womb, something the Preacher came along later and discovered, a hot fire put there by my mother and real daddy, an alive thing standing up and demanding to be accounted for, a thing the Preacher could never still, even if he pounded it a thousand times with that long wooden cross of his, so many times that the end of the cross would begin to be hot, and he would have to quit for fear of the flames turning the wood black, and creeping up the board and destroying the beginnings of everything he had based his life on.

When someone knocked on the door, Mr. Willis put a paper between us on the desk, pointed at marks there and called, "Come in," smiling at the teacher who stood there.

That afternoon we did it for the first time. We went back to the green spot in the woods, and Mr. Willis made a soft bed of big crunchy sweet gum leaves for me to lie down on. As the brown leaves drifted down from his arms full of them, he kept looking and looking at me, his mouth glistening wet and soft. We started off with our hands all over each other, touching everywhere we had wanted to touch. I felt like the waters were rushing wide open, and I opened my legs and held out my arms to the sky, and it was like there was no tightness, no holding back, but smooth, easy, free-riding, flowing, flying through the air like jumping from a high place and falling free, the air flowing past. In my head I thought I screamed, and I opened my eyes to look at Mr. Willis to see if he had heard.

But when I did, I wished I hadn't. His arms were stiff, holding him up, and he was working, sweating, staring into space, no more aware of me than if I had been a tree stump. He was not with me but was only to himself, far away to himself. Over his shoulder I could see the sky and a thin sliver of bird, sailing and swooping. As Mr. Willis let his weight fall, I felt pinned to the ground. He didn't move for a long time, and when he finally rolled off me, I started to cry.

That night while we were eating supper, some people came to the Mission. The Preacher put down his fork, and his eyes lit up. I was glad because I wasn't up to fooling with him.

When I went to bed, I tried not to think about what had

happened to me. It was like my heart was in two parts. One part of me felt cold and hard. That part never wanted to see Mr. Willis again but wanted, instead, to go to my mama's side of the bed and beg her to come sleep with me, to whisper in the dark everything I had done, to cup my hand around her ear and ask her to forgive me. The other side burned again, wanted him again, ready to go back to the leaves. That side told me that the Mr. Willis I had seen so distantly hovering above me was the way it was with men.

That night I heard the Preacher pour out all he had to the strangers who had driven up in an old beat-up car. They had probably been driving around the road in the middle of an argument, maybe, had seen the Preacher's neon sign, and had wandered into the yard. It seemed to me that the whole world was heavily laden. I knew how the Preacher looked sitting there in the old rose-flowered armchair, knee to knee with a young couple.

So many times as I grew up, I had left my room, crept down the hall, passing Mama in the laundry room sorting clothes. In the Mission door, I stood and peeked to see who was there. And though over the years my hand on the knob got bigger, the carpet under my feet more worn, the part down the middle of the Preacher's head wider, the people sitting there never seemed to change. The advice the Preacher gave them was always the same.

Early in the mornings after the people had gone, the Preacher came into the kitchen where I sat eating my Cheerios out of a bowl, and he pulled a chair up next to me. He was always shiny-eyed and red-cheeked, his hair slicked down flat and glossy with oil.

"More souls saved last night, Honey," he would say to my mother as she stood at the sink, her back to us. And then, turning to me, he would say, "You remember this one thing, girl, if you don't ever remember another. Sin always looks like something pretty, but nobody in this world ever got happy from sin."

During the next few weeks after Mr. Willis and I first did it, I watched him start to draw away from me. First I saw him leaving with Marietta Huley. I was walking down the hall toward his room. My arms were full of books almost up to my chin, and I heard him laughing in his room. I smiled and started walking faster. Then as I turned the corner, I heard Marietta's voice. "Now, why would you say that, Mr. Willis?" she was saying in a high flirty voice. As I stepped in the door, I saw her hand in the middle of his chest as though they were slow-dancing.

Mr. Willis looked around at me and said, "Hello!" in his friendly way, as though he wasn't doing anything wrong. I watched as he left with her. Out the window I saw him clear a place for her on the seat, drop the box containing the journals into the back seat, and drive off with her.

By then I knew that something was happening in me that was different from anything that had ever happened in me before, different from my Baptism when the Holy Spirit came in me, different from Mr. Willis coming in me in the woods. It was as if I heard a voice, a being, in me but also apart from me, a thing I could hear and feel but couldn't control, a thing which couldn't be killed, even if I should kill it.

First I talked to Mama. I waited until one day when the Preacher wasn't there. I sat in my room on my bed. In front of me, my books were in a tumble. I heard Mama in the kitchen. The water was running at the sink, and she was humming, "The Old Rugged Cross." I imagined how it would be. It was one thing she had always warned me against more than anything else. "Boys say they love you," she said, "just to get one thing. Don't ever fall for it if a boy asks you to prove your love."

Mr. Willis never asked that, and Mr. Willis wasn't a boy. But I had to pretend he was. I sat there and tried to convince myself. With my eyes closed, I rocked back and forth, feeling under my legs the pattern of the chenille bedspread. I tried to convince myself that a boy my own age had gotten me pregnant. I tried to picture how he would look. He was blonde or brunette and had a baby face and freckles on his nose. He was a football player and wore a blue and gold jersey. He had big muscles under his shirt. He was a member of the band and played the clarinet. He went to his car after he got out of band practice. His name was Joe or Harold or Butch. He had a mama and a daddy at home.

"Mama, I have to tell you something," I imagined myself saying. But when I opened my eyes, I was still in my room. Mama was still in the kitchen, soapsuds padding her elbows over the sink. My books were still scattered in front of me on the bed. I had not yet walked down the hall. Mama was still happy, not knowing. In minutes, everything would change.

Mama helped me to tell the Preacher. After we told him, he sat quiet for a long time in the Mission. Thinking the worst was over, I went to my room. I was curled in the middle of my bed trying to concentrate on trigonometry when he appeared in my door and said "Who?" in a booming voice.

I looked up and shook my head. "I can't say," I said.

When he took one step forward into my room, I said, "Don't start anything now. I won't tell you, no matter what you do."

When he left, I pressed my hands to my eyes and felt like a person tied to a chair in the middle of a great big field.

In the middle of the night I heard the scraping of the cross against the bottom of the trailer. It sounded like a big sleeping animal of some kind was waking up under the floor. I saw the black shadow flash across the ceiling of my room. When I pulled up on my knees to the window, the Preacher was in the middle of the street, walking up and down.

When I quit school, Mr. Willis found out and came over to our house to do the right thing. The Preacher married us, and the principal of the school came out and fired Mr. Willis later that same day.

Now Alice and I are lying side by side on the quilt. Mr. Willis is making up a song or a poem. He is tapping his fingers rhythmically on the chair arm. He asks me to think of a word that rhymes with *never*. I tell him *clever* and *forever*. Alice grabs my finger and squeezes it hard.

"Significant Loss"

SIGNIFICANT LOSS

I. Cortical Blindness

At first you saw spiders from the corner of your eye, a flicker of something black and leg-like, enough to make you turn your head and start. Next came flashing lights shooting from the left, zooming toward the right, or from above, aiming straight down.

The coffee in a cereal bowl; the Christmas tree, simply lights on a tree; the poinsettia, only red and a plant; the unassembled coffee pot, a metal stick and a basket; the towels stacked neatly in the fridge beside the milk; the clock, numbers in a circle.

The doctor said your brain couldn't tell your eyes what they saw. He asked you to write a sentence. You wrote, "Show me how to live as long as I possibly can."

"Fine," he said, as if you had written, "See Spot Run."

You said, "I think God's getting ready for me."

"He can't have you yet," I said, shielding my eyes.

II. For You, Returning

You died in the hospital room, your eyes open to something I couldn't see, your hands folded willingly across your chest. I rubbed your legs and arms, willing the warmth to stay. Later, I asked you to come back, to come inside my Self and make me you—your patience, your faithfulness, your love of the Eucharist, your willingness to plow on, no matter what. You can get used to hanging if you do it long enough, you said.

Instead, you sent a perfect slender mockingbird, its neck broken, lying on the step for me to find, completely still, one yellow-rimmed eye open wide, the other half-closed, winking, still warm, its body soft and giving. I wrapped it in a white tissue shroud and cradled it in my palm, its feet folded against its breast, submissive. You've come, I whispered.

III. Touch

In the weeks that followed, it was touch I needed most. My arms and legs tingled, desperate for some outside coming forth to surround, hover, breathe, close in. I dropped into the death chair, its back strong, its arms wanting leaning. In the yard, heat spread wide wings and settled, the sun a body, a breast, something I could put my face into. Manicure, chiropractor, pedicure, massage, all brought hands to me. Close your eyes. Hold your palm up so that I can read between the lines.

There are the hard things—the sidewalk, the table, the brick wall, the touches of a lifetime. The soft cotton above Daddy's waist, the tucking in, Mama's hand on the quilt outlining the nearly sleeping body. The lostness of them all, leaving more and more space between me, between thee, the long, long airness. How long, I long, I long for the laying on of hands.

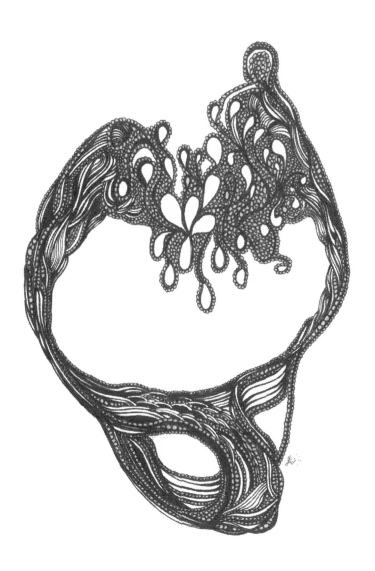

"The Washer's Husband"

THE WASHER'S HUSBAND

"More than mother and son, they were accomplices in solitude."

---Gabriel Garcia Marquez

I manage the sporting goods store at the Milledgeville Mall. My work does not take a lot of my time. Most people who come in my store know exactly what they want when they come in, I sell it to them, and they are on their way. What I sell more of than anything is jogging shorts. Joggers run through, bounce in place, and jog away, around the fountain and to the parking lot, in their hands the crisp sack of new colors rattling. My store is named "Good Sports."

Most of the time I stand on the line between my store and the tee shirt shop next door, "Heavenly Tees." I watch the people walk up and down the mall. In my head I make up stories about the people I see. Sometimes the other clerks come over and tell me about themselves. It is interesting to me to listen to people's lives and try to figure out what they mean. So far, I have heard stories from Sue at the peanut shop, Mary-Alice at the Record Bar, Laureen at the snack shop, Cricket from the bookstore, Mrs. Mayzees from the shoe store, and Nell Acree from fabrics at Penney's. Sometimes if I catch one of these people alone, I ask them about their lives. Most people think I am a good listener.

Lately Henry, who runs the tee shirt shop, has been telling me a story about his wife. It has occurred to him that Vivian washes too much. It seems to him that she washes more than other people's wives wash. For this reason, Henry tells me, he has gotten himself a lawyer to see if he can get a divorce.

"Why can't you not wash tonight?" he asks her.

"I don't know," she answers. "It's something to do."

"Will you wash every day for the rest of our lives?" he asks her.

He looks down the mall at the people walking. I look behind me into my store. A freckle-legged woman and a boy are at the counter. The boy has put a coach's whistle around his neck. I am afraid that he will blow it.

"What did she say?" I ask Henry.

"Her face became a veil," he answers.

The boy blows the whistle. The people walking stop, startled, and look both ways.

Henry says Vivian doesn't want to work outside the home. It takes away from her washing, and she has no time to finish. If she could do exactly as she wants, he says, she would get up every morning, eat the eggs and bacon he prepares for her, and she would begin. She would take the sheets from the bed and the towels from the bathroom. She would fill the washing machine. As she listened to the back-and forth-sudsing motion, I can imagine her humming a cleaning song. She would stand and listen as foaming sudsing-bubbles did their pop-pop thing. Her nostrils would fill with the cleaning smell, and she would breathe deeply and smile. She would also clean rooms—the kitchen, the bathroom. Her hand would hold the sponge, and as she stood in a chair to reach the corners, the soap would drip from her elbow to the counter top.

Henry has begun to make up slogans and put them on his tee shirts, front and back, so people can read them coming and going. His latest says "Wash me" on the front and "Whiter than Snow" on the back. All the born-again Christians from the college clamor for them. Henry begins to believe he has a special gift. At night he sits in the large blue-flowered armchair in their living room and makes up slogans while staring at the back of his wife's knees as she stuffs bundles into the washing machine.

When Henry first saw Vivian, across the room at a party their freshman year, he thought she was the cutest girl he had ever seen. She was holding a glass and looking into it, jiggling it and trying to unjumble the ice cubes to keep them from touching one another. Her eyes were hidden by her straight blond hair, which hung in wisps around her face and brushed the edges of the glass. When he touched her shoulder, she looked up, startled. He saw his reflection in her light gray eyes.

"Alone?" he asked.

"Yes," she said and began to need him.

"When I first knew her," he tells me, "she was like someone trapped in a car wreck, and I wanted to get her out." They began to go regularly to the Plow Boy for onion rings. He didn't know then that wives could reveal things that girlfriends never could. His mother had always been the same.

All his life his mother had tried to commit suicide. She tried everything—razor blades, pills, gas. The sink, Henry says, turned pink with his mother's blood. She got into the car and drove into things— trees, telephone poles, off shoulders. His daddy, tall and thin and red-faced, stood by, his arms folded, and reached out, taking her hand and lifting her up at the last moment.

Once, at the top of a hill, she closed her eyes and took her hands off the wheel. At the bottom the car hit the biggest pile of leaves she ever saw. She sat with leaves in her mouth and nose, her forehead pressed against the steering wheel. Later, sitting on a tiny stool in the corner of the kitchen as his mother fried chicken, Henry remembered how he had sat on his red tricycle and watched her walking back up the hill, leaves in her hair, in her shoes, and in her fists. In the kitchen, leaning his chin on his knee, he picked from the black-and-white octagon-shaped tiles a brown leaf beside his foot. When he put it in his mouth and chewed it up, it tasted like his mother's life.

Henry tells me that every night his wife goes to sleep on the floor in front of the television, her cheek molded into the carpet, her glasses pressed into her nose. He calls and calls her. "Vivian! Wake up!" When she finally sits up, startled, she shouts at him, "I was not asleep!" Then she goes to remove the warm clothes from the dryer.

She keeps a washcloth beside the bed. Every night she replaces it with a new one, clean and fresh from the dryer. She wets it in the bathroom sink, squeezes it, and folds it neatly on a plate which she leaves under the edge of the pink bedspread fringe on her side. At night when he has finished reading his mystery book and turns out the light, she slips the cloth to him quietly in the dark. "Here," she says. "Wipe your hands." She first hands him the washcloth, then puts his hand on a breast or the soft inside of a thigh.

I tell him something does not sound right about so much washing. He tells me he wants a wife he can feel safe about having children with.

When Henry was nine, his daddy built him a jungle gym.

Standing at his daddy's knees, he watched as his daddy ran the loud saw, the wood chips piling up on the ground. In the dark of the kitchen doorway stood Henry's mother, her white apron shining through the screen. When the saw slowed to a whine, the two of them heard her call, "Don't stand too close! Those chips can fly loose and put your eye out." Henry remembers looking up at his father and saying, "We're not afraid, are we?"

The jungle gym had rope swings, ladders, and high rafters on which to climb. It could be dangerous if you weren't a big boy and knew what to do. Sometimes when he went inside, Henry could see out the bathroom window his mother walking around and around his jungle gym. Then she stood, her brow lowered, and looked at it, rubbing her chin. Remembering it now, Henry makes up a new slogan. On the front he writes, "Danger"; on the back, "Swinging Bridge" or "Low Flying Objects."

The next night, after three wash loads of clothes, Henry confronts Vivian about her washing. When in bed she holds out the washcloth to him, he says, "No. My hands are clean." She kicks him hard, and her toenail cuts his leg. He gets up and snatches the cloth, dangling it over her head. She dances like a puppet, loose and frail, her blue-flowered gown billowing like an angel dress. She reaches up and cries, "Give me back my washcloth. I hate you with all my heart."

Remembering it, Henry tells me he thinks he was laughing. He thinks he carried his point too far. He left her at home on the sofa, curled into a ball, her thumb in her mouth. He does not feel proud of his actions. Sometimes he wants to squeeze her and make her whole. He wants to take that ache out of her and put it in the back yard and set fire to it. I ask if he has considered taking her to a doctor. He thinks about it for two weeks and then decides that I am right.

The doctor tells her to hold her arms out straight in front of her, palms upturned. He asks her one question: "How long have you been sad?" She puts her face in her hands and begins to sob.

"It seems that nobody loves me...," she says.

"Certainly your husband...," says the doctor.

"Not enough," says the Washer, shaking her head.

It was then that the doctor asks Henry to wait outside. After thirty minutes, Vivian and the doctor open the door and approach Henry, who sits cross-legged in a red velour chair, reading *Psychology Today*. "I think Vivian needs to spend a couple of weeks in our hospital," the doctor says. "We need to do some tests." Vivian stands beside him, her head down. She doesn't look at Henry, and Henry doesn't look at her.

During the time Vivian is at the hospital, I visit her twice. I don't know her but think it would mean a lot to Henry. He tells me she likes to read biographies of women. He says she is looking for someone to be like. At the bookstore I pick out Loretta Lynn and Marilyn Monroe and wrap them in pink paper. When I walk into Vivian's room and hold them out to her, she takes them from my hand and looks into my eyes. I could be anybody. When I leave, she clings to me.

The second time, her grandparents are there too. We sit around a table in the coffee shop. Her grandfather, an old freckled man in a gray hat and plaid shirt, puts his hand on Vivian's head and says, "There ain't nothing wrong that a couple of weeks on my farm won't cure." When Vivian comes home, she brings Henry a leather belt she has made and me a small bookcase that holds six books.

A week later Henry tells me that the dryer did not go off until four a.m. and that he is bushed. He does not think he can go through this all his life. He wants something to look forward to, not those long, long stretches. He wants to have children.

Two days later Henry announces to the Washer that he wants a divorce because the marriage is not working and because he does not love her the way a husband should love a wife. There is more to a relationship than not arguing, he says. Vivian says, "You are ruining my life. You are spoiling all my plans."

When he gets home that afternoon, he finds that something has happened. The Washer has taken the scissors and begun pruning. She has pruned the cord on the video-recorder for which Henry saved for months. She has pruned Henry's mystery books, his house robe, the record covers to his Linda Ronstadt and Willie Nelson albums, and the tongues from his shoes.

When he sees her holding the scissors in her hand like a protest sign, he calls the police before she prunes the telephone cord.

When the police arrive, they have on their faces an expression that says "Domestic Squabble." They look from Henry to Vivian and back again and say, "If this ever happens again, somebody's going to get locked up."

That night Vivian washes all the sheets and towels and window curtains and antimacassars and throw rugs. She begins at one end of her closet and moves to the other, washing many colored blouses, skirts, pants, and dresses. Hangers empty from the left and fill from the right with clean clothes. The room fills with the smell of Downy. At five a.m. she crawls into bed with Henry and puts her arms around him, waking him. Her tears fall on his cheeks and on the back of his neck. "I am so sorry," she says again and again. "Please, my darling, forgive me." With her fingertips she smooths the hair at the nape of his neck.

As Henry dresses for work, he discovers that she has cut the sleeves from his red "Members Only" jacket. And on the hood of his silver Toyota are her initials in big sprawling scratches.

Henry's lawyer tells him he cannot move out. If he moves, she will take him for everything he's got. That afternoon he takes all his mystery books and records and moves into the small guest room, locking the door behind him. From inside, he sees the toe of her shoe as she kicks. Her shoe makes a hole she can peep through while lying on the carpet, her head propped on her elbow. He pushes a chair against the door.

In the middle of the night Henry hears her whimpering, "I didn't mean to do those things to you." Henry stumbles across the dark room. He moves the chair. He turns the key and opens the door a crack. She stands there in her long white gown. He takes her hand, and she curls onto the floor with him. He sees his reflection in her eyes.

"My mother was not as crazy as that," he says to me.

The next day Henry finds that she has emptied the drawer which contained his rock from the Grand Canyon, his Bruce Lee medal, his Creative Writing Award, and his last three cat's-eye marbles. He takes the Washer by the shoulders and shakes her. Her hair falls into her face. "I would never have thrown away your memory books," he says to her.

"I don't know why I did it," she says and begins to cry.

Henry makes up a slogan. On the front he has drawn a blank surrounded by quotation marks; on the back, the word *Etc.*

Now Henry is quiet. He comes to work and stands in the doorway as before. He looks down the mall and, like me, watches the people come and go. He has stopped going to the lawyer, and I have stopped asking him about the Washer.

I have been standing in my store trying to figure out what Henry's life means. I imagine Henry's father standing on a hill beside Henry. Henry sits on his red tricycle. Together they watch Henry's mother ride the car down the hill. Henry's hand is around his father's leg at the knee, his father's hand on Henry's hair. Again and again she trudges up the hill and goes to the kitchen to fry chicken. Each time she drops leaves behind her as she walks. On Saturday mornings she vacuums them up again. And all the way from the top of the hill to the kitchen and back again, Henry and his father talk softly to one another.

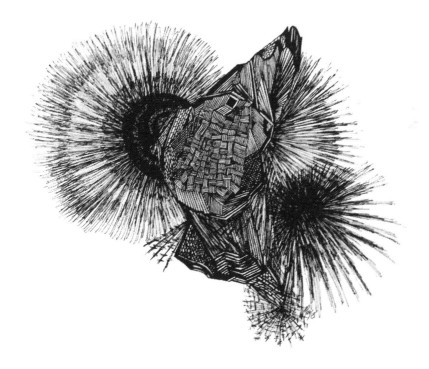

"The Ola Dress"

THE OLA DRESS

"Some of us aren't meant to belong. Some of us have to turn the world upside down and shake the hell out of it until we make our own place in it."

--Elizabeth Lowell

I chose Kathy to give The Ola Dress to. I thought she was the most sentimental of all the second cousins. I remembered her as a child, her sweet smile, her loving ways. Everyone always said she was the grandchild most like Aunt Alice, my mother's oldest sister. Kathy was the one who sent birthday cards to Mama and pictures of her children in Christmas cards every year.

It was the night before she died from ovarian cancer that Mama told me about The Ola Dress. It was the night she wanted to talk, and she wanted me to take notes about everything she said. I sat in a chair at the foot of her bed with a notepad and pen.

"The family pictures are in that second drawer to my desk in the living room," she said. "Separate those by family and give them to whichever family they belong. That gold Depression glass bowl with the roses in the bottom is something Alice brought me from the World's Fair. You can keep it."

She waved her hand in the air over her face as if shooing away a bug. Then she continued. "There is an old dress in the bottom drawer of my dresser. We always called it The Ola Dress because it belonged to a cousin of ours who died young. We got her dress, and Alice tatted a neckline to run a ribbon through. You might want to put that in a shadow box."

Then she got philosophical. "Life is a book, and this is the grand finale," she said. And, "It is as important to prepare for death as it is to prepare for life." And, "Don't hold anything against anybody, whatever they did or didn't do during this time of my sickness." And, finally, "Is everything all right? Between us?"

Ironic that she would ask that last question. It was the question I always asked her, the question I asked to make that gnawing feeling of guilt, or something not being right, go away. A feeling that the radio station was not quite on the mark, a sound of static inside my heart. The question was always brought on by that look on my mother's face, the sad look, the look that made me think I had done something wrong, made her mad, hurt her feelings.

So often I had. If I talked back or touched something in the store after being told not to so many times, there was that look, the sad look. And the waiting began. Waiting for forgiveness. It seemed like hours, the back turned, the silence, the look, that look.

"Mama, smile when I smile," I said, looking up at her, the tips of my fingers touching her elbow as she stood staring out the window over the kitchen sink.

"I don't feel like smiling," she said.

"Is everything all right yet?" I asked, after waiting longer.

If everything wasn't all right yet, the answer was silence.

"Mama, I'm sorry," I pleaded.

"There are some things that saying 'I'm sorry' won't make all right," she said. When she said that, I wondered what those things might be. What could you do that could not be undone? You could kill a person. Saying 'I'm sorry' would not bring a dead person back to life. I wondered if my mother thought I would ever commit a murder. When she said those words, life seemed like a long tunnel of waiting with something beautiful only at the end, something like blue light, like pink quartz, like forgiveness.

What Mama wanted to know that night was if that never-again-mentioned subject was still standing between us, or if it had been finally put to rest. It was a subject I would not discuss again, not on that night, or the next day, or ever again with my mother.

It was the day that, once happened, was put to rest, buried between us as real as if it had been given a bonafide funeral and had been buried in a coffin under layers of dirt. It was the day, followed by the next day, the day of declaration followed by the day of about-face, of turn-around, of the renunciation of the declaration.

"Mama, I want to go live with Gale," I said in the letter I handed her at age twenty-eight, on the day I had designated to tell her in her living room. "She makes me happy, and I love her," I wrote in my leaning-backward handwriting.

The letter that day slipped from my mother's fingers. It fluttered to the floor like a wounded bird. My mother's face went into her hands. She shook her head. The tears came. "I can't live here in this town any more," she said. "I'm going to have to move."

I can't explain what happened to me in my bed that night in my apartment alone. All I know is that the next morning, nothing in my life was the same. I could not do the deed. I could not move ahead, my mother's life ruined. The feeling had to go away. That was all. I promised God that I would never kiss another woman.

The next morning meant one phone call to my mother. "Never mind," I said. "It's not going to happen. I take it back."

All I said to Gale was, "I'm sorry, but I can't."

From that day on, I became the person that I could live with. My mother and I never referred to that day again. Until that night and the question she asked. "Is everything all right? Between us?"

"Absolutely," I said.

I understand the short story, "Story of an Hour" by Kate Chopin. The woman whose husband dies and who pulls her chair to the window and imagines herself doing all the things in her life that she has never been able to do because her husband was alive. And I am not one to question Chopin, but I have always thought that story should have ended with the woman sitting with her chair at the window. That was all that was needed, the woman realizing that she was free, not the husband, not dead after all, walking into the house and spoiling all her newly-made plans.

I met Lauren on match.com, and we were married in Vermont. The day I went to meet Kathy at the Mexican restaurant in Eatonton, I took my wedding pictures. I had put them in an album, and I was filled with the zeal and confidence of a new convert. Kathy was young and hip. She would be cool with the news.

I left The Ola Dress in the car when I went into the restaurant. It was big and was in a shadow box with a glass front and a large, cumbersome wooden frame. In my arm I held the album containing mine and Lauren's wedding pictures.

Kathy looked like a hippy. She had on a soft cotton peasant

shirt in colors of purple and green. Her long brownish-graying braid hung like a rope over her left shoulder.

"I'm so glad you told me," she said, turning the pages of our album. "Now I can relax," she said. "Now I can really hug you." A strange statement, but I thought I understood. It meant, "Now I really know you."

When we went to our cars after lunch, we moved The Ola Dress from my trunk to hers. She seemed pleased to have it.

It wasn't until before the family reunion that I learned that Kathy had told everyone. All my first cousins, her parents, who then told their brothers and sisters. Soon all my first cousins in Atlanta—all of Aunt Alice's children—had been told that I had married a woman. All these cousins, Fundamentalist Baptists, who had surely voted against Obama. "I didn't even know two women could get married," Kathy said that her mother, my cousin Patsy, had said. Kathy had many excuses about why she had told them: it was an accident; she had let something slip about how happy she was for me, and then Patsy wouldn't let it drop until she told her. Patsy told her husband Buster. Buster called up Larry and Frankie. Larry called up Bertha and Bob. In less than a day, all of Aunt Alice's children and their husbands and wives and Milledgeville knew. But I went to the family reunion anyway. I was determined finally to live my own life.

At the reunion Kathy had an album of her own. She was proud to show me the pictures from hers and her husband Dale's hunting trip to Africa. I sat down and turned the pages. There on every page, one after the other, were pictures of Kathy with her rifle by her side, genuflecting beside the corpse of a dead animal, its feet folded as if in prayer. There she was on every page, posed the same way, smiling the same smile, her long gray braid hanging over her shoulder, proud that she was a real woman who knew how to shoot and kill beautiful animals. She was at the family get-together, but she was not proud of her casserole; she was proud of her album. Zebra, antelope, caribou, wildebeest. Page after page of carnage. Why would you kill a zebra? I was thinking as I turned the pages. I was not thinking, Now I can really hug you.

Before we left, Kathy said, "You and Lauren must come and

see our house. All the animals have come in, and we have them on the wall. I don't know how you feel about early dead animal." She laughed. "Well, I'm thinking that The Ola Dress probably doesn't fit in with the décor," I said.

"Not really," she said. "I gave it to Daddy, and he has it on the wall in the basement. It looks good down there."

I pictured it. The Ola dress encased in glass, protected, waiting, ready to be passed down through the generations, the leftover from a dead girl, frozen in place, something that probably wouldn't fit in anywhere.

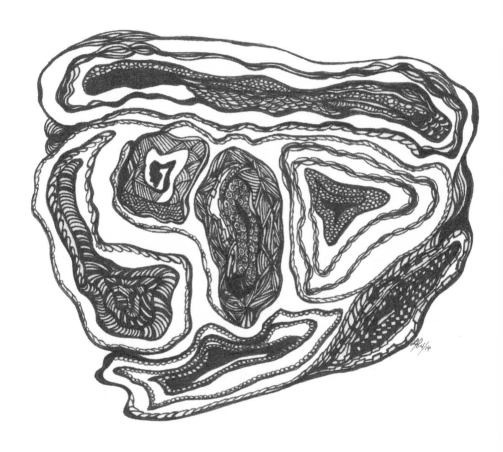

"Buster's Night Out"

BUSTER'S NIGHT OUT

"All the lonely people, where do they all come from?"

--Eleanor Rigby, The Beatles

When Buster Bloodworth, wearing his baby-blue pajamas, left the Milledgeville Veterans Home and showed up at his sister Alma's front door at six in the evening, no one knew what to do with him. Alma was talking on the telephone to her friend, Frances Ruth. She held the telephone to her ear and peered languidly through the white ruffled sheers drawn across the window, twisting the black telephone cord, and watching red, green, and orange cars zoom past on the highway outside.

"Sure is hot," she said to Frances Ruth. "Thought I'd sit on the screened-in porch, but I declare it's too hot to move from the oscillating fan."

It was then that she heard the tapping on the door. Alma told Frances Ruth to hold on a minute because it might be a rapist. "If I don't come back," she told her, "you hang up and call the police."

Buster pressed his nose and hands against the screen, his blond hair standing up on top like the crest of a pale brown flycatcher. When Alma's silhouette in her red-flowered housedress moved down the dark hall, he cried silently, his shoulders heaving.

"Oh, it's you, Buster," Alma said. She let him in and followed him down the hall to the kitchen. He slid his feet three inches at a time like a wind-up toy unknowingly walking off the edge of a table or a chair arm.

"Now stop crying, Brother," Alma said behind him. "What are you doing out? Who let you out? Was it Fernie?"

He turned himself slowly in a circle and sat backwards into the gray plastic dinette chair. "I called me a taxi-cab and left. I'm not going back." His voice was so low that Alma could barely hear him. "I'm going to get me one of them apartments at Dogwood Village and live there until I die. You can check every day to see if I've gone yet."

"Holy Mary, deliver me from this," said Alma to herself as she remembered the telephone and ran to the other room.

"Frances Ruth? You still there? It's Buster." She cupped her hands around her mouth and whispered loudly into the phone. "I don't know what I'm going to do. Bernice is working tonight. I'm not able to keep him. He's too heavy, and he wets himself."

"Call Evangeline," suggested Frances Ruth, who had known their family from the beginning.

Ignoring her, Alma continued. "I knew something bad was coming this afternoon when I took a nap on the couch. I had a nightmare, and I woke up soaked through."

"It certainly has been hot," said Frances Ruth. "I don't know why Buster wanted to leave that nice air-conditioned building and come out in this heat."

Alma dragged the phone to her dressing table and stood arranging her gray curls as she talked. "I dreamed I went into the church to fix the flowers and found the statue of the Blessed Mother stuffed down in the garbage can, her head sticking out."

"Well, that was strange," said Frances Ruth. "That's the reason I can't take naps in the middle of the afternoon."

"Father was there," said Alma, "and he kept saying, 'This is the Madonna of the Garbage, this is the Madonna of the Garbage.' It was awful. I knew then that something bad was going to happen today." She dragged the phone to the kitchen door and looked in at Buster who appeared to have fallen asleep in the chair.

"If it was me, I'd call Evangeline," Frances Ruth said again. "Evangeline never has done right by your family that I can tell."

What Frances Ruth said was true. Evangeline never had done anything. She was spoiled all her life. Back home, every time Mama and Papa needed water from the well or a chicken killed or the yard swept, it was always Alma or Bernice who had to go do it. It was never Buster or Evangeline. Petted. Always petted. It seemed as though Mama and Papa were scared of them, Alma thought.

She could see why, too. She didn't relish calling up Evangeline and being told to go to hell. That was what Evangeline and Buster did to get their way. It seemed that they had a streak of the devil in them from the beginning.

Evangeline's daughter, Gladys, and Gladys's husband, T.A., catered to Evangeline. Gladys and T.A. couldn't even have T.A.'s family over for lunch without Evangeline feeling left out and calling up. "Just want to let you know I'm all right," she said, and T.A. would get up from the table and go out to the country to get her.

Buster was the same way. Always petted and never had to lift a finger. But he wouldn't have become an alcoholic if the Spear brothers hadn't thrown him down at twelve midnight the night the war ended and poured Rebel Yell down his throat. From that night on, Buster carried a brown paper sack with him wherever he went.

When Buster came home from the war, his wife waited on him hand and foot. His daughter, Fernie, who never spoke to him, called him a drunken bastard behind his back. Alma couldn't understand it. Her own father.

When Buster's wife died, that was it. The only tie between Buster and Fernie gone.

Now Buster was here in Alma's kitchen crying and whining that he had ruined his life, and it was too late for him to fix it.

When Evangeline answered the phone, Alma said, "Evangeline, Buster's out. He's come over here, and I'm not able to keep him. I'm going to bring him out to your house. You're as capable as I am."

"Damn," Evangeline answered and slammed the receiver in Alma's ear.

Alma walked through the kitchen, past Buster with his head in his hands, to the window. Pulling back the curtains, she looked out. In the garage was her '57 Chevrolet, its back bumper covered with bird droppings.

The phone rang. "I'm the oldest in the family," said Evangeline.

"You're healthier than the rest of us," said Alma.

"But I don't drive," whined Evangeline.

"T.A. takes you anywhere you need to go," said Alma.

"But Buster's not T.A.'s family," said Evangeline.

"He's your own brother, Evangeline. Now I'm bringing him out there, and you're going to have to do your duty by him."

"Well, certainly, I'm used to it. I'm always the one that gets the bad end of the stick."

"You can go on all you want, Evangeline. I'm bringing him."

"Go to hell," was the answer.

When Alma returned to the kitchen, Buster was smoking, dropping ashes on the front of his pajamas.

"That's another thing that makes it hard for us, Buster. You're going to burn the house down one night."

Buster tried to say something. Alma leaned close. "I do the best I can," he whispered. "I'm thirsty."

"I know. I know." She patted his round shoulder.

"I'm not going back," he said. "I'm going to get me an apartment."

"Where is Fernie? How can I find Fernie?" asked Alma as she tied an apron around her waist and put a boiler of water over the burner to make coffee.

He didn't answer. She turned, her hands in the pockets of the apron. Shaking his head, he answered hoarsely, "I took her name off the checking account. I think she's going to move to Needmore."

When Alma pulled her '57 Chevrolet into Evangeline's yard, Evangeline, T.A., and Gladys were standing on the front porch in a row. T.A.'s red Ford station wagon was parked under the pecan tree.

T.A. came over to the car and helped Buster into the back seat of the station wagon. Glowering at Alma, he said, "I'm taking him home with me, but he ain't my kin."

As Alma drove home, the hot, dusty air beat her face. A large black insect flew directly into the windshield, its yellow insides splatting on the glass in the shape of a star that she couldn't see through.

That night Alma dreamed she was back home in bed with Mama. In her dream she tried to say something to Mama, but the words wouldn't come. "It seemed like it was a confession," she had said. "It was a confession I was trying to remember."

"Yes, yes, those confessions," her mother had answered in her dream. "Always those confessions from my Alma in the middle of the night."

When we were young, Alma thought the next morning as she

leaned her elbows on the table, sin was a terrible burden. You had to have somebody to confess to.

My brother is too heavy for me, she thought, and it seemed like a sin. But it wasn't the kind of sin to confess to the priest. It was the kind she wanted to confess to Mama. Her head on Mama's feather pillow. He's too heavy for all of us, Mama.

She put her coffee cup into the sink and walked to the front window to watch the cars zip by, separating her from Tip's Market across the street. The price of lettuce was thirty-nine cents a head. Do you hear me, Lord? Praying made things easier, Alma thought.

That was Evangeline's problem. She had never been able to pray. When Mama and Papa carried them to Mass when they were little, Evangeline stood beside Mama and held her hand. When the priest said the words of the consecration over the Host, Evangeline whispered, "What's he doing now, Mama?"

Mama leaned close to her and said, "He's changing the bread into God."

"But I don't believe in God," Evangeline whined.

"Hush, Honey," Mama said.

When the priest opened the door of the tabernacle, Evangeline whispered, "What now?"

"He's putting God back into His house. See? That's God's house."

"But I don't believe in God," Evangeline insisted and stomped her foot.

Mama pulled Evangeline's head close to her bosom and whispered, "Don't say that, darling. Remember, your name is Evangeline."

Buster wouldn't go to church. Mama and Papa made him go for a while. But he broke loose from Mama's arm and ran down the aisle until Mama cried from embarrassment.

After Buster came home from the war, he was Somebody. He sold insurance, joined the Country Club, and wore his red blazer.

He wasn't Buster then, either. He was George Albert. George Albert Bloodworth. He played golf every Sunday afternoon, moving gracefully across the lawn, laughing with friends. Somebody, the twisted end of the brown sack sticking out of his pocket.

"That you, Buster?" Alma remembered. It was an old joke a friend told at one of their family reunions. "That you, Buster?"

Myrtice Acre had been waiting at the Medical Center, reading a story in True Confessions when the nurse called out, "George Albert Bloodworth. Next. George Albert Bloodworth."

"Well," said Myrtice, "I saw this tall fellow in a red jacket get up and go to the door, and I says to myself, 'Blest if that ain't Buster Bloodworth.'"

"'That you, Buster?' I said. I wish you could of seen him. He turned right then and there from George Albert Bloodworth into Buster. Right before my eyes."

Buster walked away from these stories and sat in his green Buick where Alma knew his brown paper bag was under the seat.

Fernie was not Somebody. Fernie had made up her mind to become a full time hippy. It made Alma sick every time she thought about Fernie's mother and how hurt she would be at the way Fernie had turned out.

Fernie's mother was a real lady, fancy clothes in her closet from end to end. But Fernie wouldn't have any of her mama's clothes. She spent the money on foolishness and let herself go to pot. That is what Alma found out the last time Buster left the Veterans Hospital, and she had gone to find Fernie.

She knew where Fernie lived then because of the purple Volkswagen van she'd bought to carry her St. Bernard dogs around in. The noise of the record player was so loud that Alma had to bang on the door.

"I'm not ever going to be free as long as I've got him around my neck," Fernie had yelled over the noise.

"But he's your father, Fernie," Alma had told her.

"Don't you start that, Aunt Alma. You don't know what it was like. He is a load around my neck. He may as well be engraved across my chest. All my life I've been able to remember the number on his dog tag in the army. I used to hold my hand over the radio so Mama could pick up the news. I can recite that number today. Seven—two—eight—four—nine—four—three."

Alma had stood at the front door of Fernie's apartment and looked at the girl whose frizzy hair stood out in all directions, who didn't look like a girl at all, and remembered the blond beauty presented to Fernie's mother years ago in the hospital at Needmore.

Bernice or somebody else would have to look for Fernie this time. She wasn't going to do it.

"That you, Buster?" The phone rang, and Alma put the receiver to her ear. She could barely hear a soul. "That you, Buster?"

"T.A.'s called the Dogwood Village." It was Buster's wheeze. "T.A.'s called the Dogwood Village and told them that I'll smoke in bed and burn the apartments down. They won't take me."

"Give me the phone." It was T.A. "Alma, listen. I can't keep Buster here. He smokes in the bed. He wets the sheets. The whole damn house smells like him. I don't have to keep him when he ain't my kin."

"You married Gladys, T.A. You can't be kin and not be kin. You got to take us all," Alma answered.

"I'm bringing him back. Bernice will be home soon, and the two of you will have to work it out."

"What about Evangeline?" Alma asked.

"Evangeline is Gladys' mother. I'm not going to put her through this."

By the time Bernice got home, T.A. had brought Buster and left him sitting in the living room. Alma paced the floor in front of him, walking from the back window where she could see her Chevrolet in the garage to the front window where the cars passed by.

"I'm thirsty," Buster kept saying. "I'm so thirty."

"You've always been thirsty," said Bernice, who sat in the chair, knitting. "Get you a glass of water."

"Water don't help," wheezed Buster.

"Your liver is ruined," said Alma. "Your heart's weak. Your legs are shriveled, and you can hardly talk. How can you ask for something besides water?"

"Water don't satisfy me," said Buster.

"Your problem is that you've never been to Mass," said Bernice, without looking up from her knitting.

It was then that Fernie burst into the room wearing a turquoise blue tee shirt that said, "I'm a virgin and proud of it" in a big black letters across her bosom. Two St. Bernard dogs charged in behind her and ran around the room, sniffing loudly, their long wet tongues hanging out.

One of them grabbed Bernice's knitting and began to look under the couch for a place to bury it.

"Get up," Fernie said to Buster. "I'm taking you back. Go get in the van."

"I'm not going back," said Buster.

"If you don't go back today, they won't take you back. That's their rule," said Fernie.

When Alma stood to help Buster, Fernie grabbed her arm. "Leave him alone. He's not as helpless as he pretends to be."

"I'm thirsty," said Buster.

Bernice screamed and backed out from under the couch. "That dog bit me!"

"You should have left him alone," said Fernie. "You mess with other folk's things and you get bit." She slammed the door behind them and pushed Buster across the porch.

Bernice and Alma stood in the living room and looked at one another, Bernice holding her hurt hand in the crook of her arm like a baby.

"You know," said Bernice. "Everybody in this world needs them a Buster and an Evangeline."

As the van drove away, the dogs barking loudly, Alma backed out of the room into the dark hallway. Holy Jesus, how many innocents. How many blond-haired babies. Holy Mary, Madonna of the Garbage.

"It makes you realize how much you got to be thankful for," yelled Bernice from the other room.

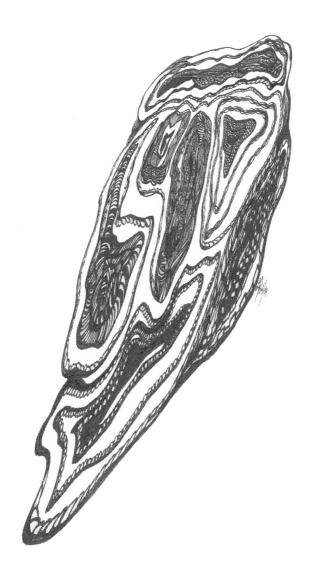

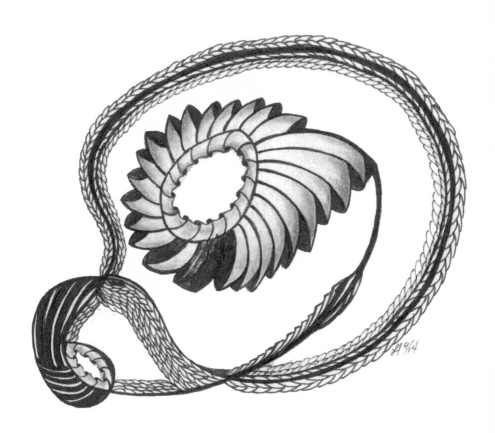

"The Hat"

THE HAT

"I myself have 12 hats, and each one represents a different personality."

--Margaret Atwood

It's a hat I need. Just a hat. If I had her hat, I could become her any time I wanted. I could put on her hat as I sat down to write, and every word that came out of my pen would be the words of my character.

That is what I am thinking the night Mama and I go out to eat at the new Milledgeville Sizzlin'. As we sit waiting for our order to arrive, I say to her, "Mama, do you still have any of your old hats?"

"Yes," she says. "Why do you ask?"

"Do you know where they are?" I ask.

"I think I do," she says. "I think some of them are on the shelf over my dresses, and a couple of others may be in the cabinet over the shower in your daddy's bathroom."

The way Mama is, she doesn't question the things I do as long as she knows I'm confiding in her. If I'm confiding in her, what I'm doing can't be wrong.

So I tell her I've got this character that is part me and part herself. I tell her that when I write, I have to be able to jump into this character's skin and become her, and that I think a hat will do the trick.

I tell her I need a hat so I can take it off and put it on again, that if I tried something more serious, something like prayer, it might become permanent. I don't want to become her permanently so that I could never be myself again.

"What kind of a hat do you want?" she asks.

I draw a picture on my napkin and slip it over to her. It is a broad-brimmed felt hat, possibly in a dark green or a fuchsia. It has a band and maybe a feather that I'll be able to see in front of me as I write.

"I don't have any hats that are tacky like that," she says.

"Oh, my character wouldn't wear a tacky hat," I say. "May I come look? And if I find one I like, do you think maybe I could have it?"

"I guess so," she says. "But I can't imagine any of my hats looking good on you with your hair cut short like that."

For some reason this gets me tickled. It seems to me that I haven't laughed this hard in a long time. I realize that I have snorted and that two men at a table near us have turned to look. They are wearing white sleeveless tee shirts, and one has a tattoo of a cross on his arm.

When I am finally able to talk, I say, "Oh! I'm not going to wear it to answer the door or to go to the grocery store."

"It will probably be too big for you," she says.

The next evening I go over to Mama's house just as it has begun to get dark. Mama is sitting on the glider on the screened porch and is wearing a yellow cotton housecoat. Around her neck is the white cotton handkerchief she wears to absorb perspiration when the weather is hot.

"Do you feel like looking for hats?" I ask her. "Is it too late? Or too hot?"

"I guess not," she says. "Go out under the carport and get that ladder. Don't bump the furniture with it."

In her back room, she props the ladder beside the closet and begins climbing up the rungs one, then two. I see her white legs, the blue veins behind her knees. On her feet are terrycloth slippers. When she is on the second rung, I say, "Let me do it."

"I just want to see if they're up here," she says. Then from the dark shelf, she starts to hand the hat boxes down to me, one by one. I put them in a row on her bed, not opening any of them yet.

Then, standing on the ladder myself, from the cabinet over Daddy's shower, I have to move two boxed wedding gowns out of the way before I can reach the last hat box.

When we have all the hat boxes lined up on the bed, I take the lids off. There are five hats: a black straw with a broad brim and a black band; a black straw with bright rose-colored flowers around the brim; a yellow straw with orange flowers around the sides; a bright pink satin shaped like a bowl; and a turquoise-blue felt with a turned-up brim and a top which comes to a point.

I immediately discard the two that have large flowers on them.

"My character wouldn't wear these flowers," I tell Mama. "They look like something her mother might wear." That leaves the solid black straw with the large flat brim, the bright pink satin, and the turquoise-blue felt.

Next I discard the pink satin—too bright. She wouldn't want to look conspicuous. She wouldn't want to stand out in a crowd. Mama says she wore that hat on Easter. It went with a suit she had which was that color.

That leaves the choice between the plain black and the turquoise felt. I look into the mirror and try on the black. I turn my head from side to side. It's okay but is nothing special. I look away and close my eyes to see how I feel in it. I imagine myself writing. I try to feel like my character. It's hard to do. I need to be alone. It's hard to imagine, with Mama standing in the room.

Then I put on the turquoise blue felt. It looks cute. I look in the mirror and turn my head from side to side. I smile. The hat has a long plastic stickpin through the crown. On the end of the pin is a ball of white pearls. "That was an expensive hat in its day," Mama says.

I can imagine myself sitting in a department store with a clerk standing behind me saying, "This is a stylish hat. It's becoming to you."

"I'm not sure it's my character," I say. "It seems a bit fancy for her. Still, I think she would be attracted to it. I don't think she would be able to resist a hat this cute. I think she might like it." I close my eyes and turn away. I smile.

"I love this hat," I say to Mama the next day on the telephone.

"It won't ever be the same again," she answers.

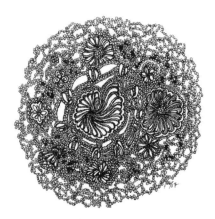

"Medusa"

MEDUSA

"Just as a snake sheds its skin, we must shed our past, again and again."

--Buddha

I was born, but I'm not dead. I am probably about three quarters there.

Until now, I have touched my mother's breasts, sitting in her lap after our baths, the water droplets on our bodies. I sat on the toilet, watching faces in the patterns on the tiles, my elbows resting on my naked knees. I imagined, in the crack between the floor and the bathtub, a snake that could emerge into the room, where I was alone. Sick with the measles, I lay in my narrow bed, the fever buzzing in my head, and imagined the girl on the calendar coming closer and closer, threatening.

I watched my daddy push the lawnmower across the grass, the inch-long green blades flying onto his back. I saw him stop, get a hoe, and strike, until one snake became many segments.

I sassed my mother and waited for her to turn around from the kitchen sink and make everything all right again. I fell in love with my seventh grade teacher; when she moved away, I cried for days, lying across my bed, until my mother said, Too much grief. She's not your mother. I watched the bluebird mother coax her babies from their nest, doing what came naturally.

I saw a snake crawl into the bluebird house and eat the eggs. A neighbor with a hoe tossed gasoline from a cup into the opening, the snake with its bulging body coming into the air, waving from side to side, vulnerable.

I heard my mother say, There are some things that saying I'm sorry won't make all right; I clung to her legs and begged, Please, please, please.

I drove over a snake in my driveway, backed up and did it again, the frantic coiling making my feet jump, my arm move the gear shift from forward to reverse more often than I intended. The next morning I found the un-dead snake resting in a flower bed, its upright head and piercing eyes questioning, Why did you?

I kissed a woman and was surprised that it was what I always wanted. Through the glass window I watched a mermaid at Weeki-Watchi Springs, her hair waving in the water, Medusa with her snakes.

I told my mother about the woman I loved, and, thinking her hurt would last forever, I didn't wait nearly long enough to be absolved.

I saw a frog sitting in the round door of a birdhouse, its webbed feet clinging for dear life.

I watched my mother's body get overtaken with ovarian cancer, swelling her abdomen to the size when I was inside. I despised the alien cells that filled the space that was once my place.

I heard my mother say, when the end was near: Is everything all right? Between us?

I felt my mother come back, and I saw a snake stretched in the sun on a fence post. I said, You go your way; I'll go mine.

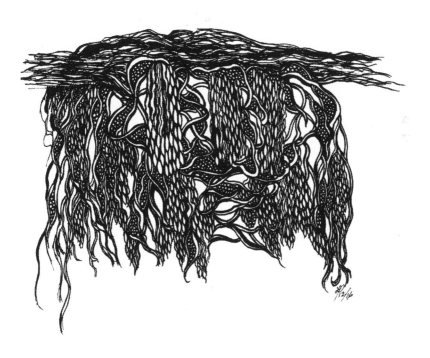

"Esther's Real People"

ESTHER'S REAL PEOPLE

"So many women just don't know how great they are. They come to us all vogue on the outside and vague on the inside."

--Mary Kay Ash, Mary Kay Cosmetics

Thank you, I'm glad to be back. No, I haven't been sick, just away. You better eat more than that. You'll get weak and not be able to put one foot in front of the other. Fix you some grits with cheese, something nourishing. Two. Three. Six for a dollar. Coupon on this? Sorry, honey, this one is expired. And wait a minute, baby, there's a limit on this one. Oh, dear, today's not your day. Got to have six before you get the discount. Double coupons tomorrow. Today ought to be tomorrow.

Well, honey, you know me. I never have asked for anything but peace and quiet and some money to fall back on. I wouldn't have up and left for no good reason. But, I swear, it sounded good. I reached a point in my life when I had to take a chance even if I failed. That was the way it was with me since that day Mrs. Lasseter came in here.

Need a price on this, darling. Thank you. Third aisle, I think. Over there with the Chinese. Those high school boys never get the foreign foods priced right. In here before daylight, then off to school. I bet they sleep through their English and math classes.

You know the kind I mean. She was a pretty lady. She came up here where you're standing now and leaned over here and—listen, I don't want everybody to hear this—leaned over and whispered in my ear, "You could be a beautiful woman," then wrote me a check on scenes of the mountains. Her pen had a mink ball bobbing on the top. She slipped me her check with a blue card stuck up under it and glided out the electric door like she owned the world.

Well, she had started something then. I went home and stood in front of the mirror and imagined it, the whole works. Shoot, you know that's not the truth, but that's how we all are. You might not, but I got a streak of vanity in my bones. All it takes is a suggestion, and I'm standing in front of the mirror thinking I'm the main character in

Camelot and on my way to Hollywood. I think we're all that way, don't you?

Where'd you get this, aisle seven? Looks like it's got a tear in it. Sweetie, run get this lady another bag of this corn meal. It's that over there on special. This one will be all over everything before she gets home.

Well, I had to call the number on that blue card, or nothing would do me. Next thing I knew, I had bought me one of those *Glamour* magazines over there, and Mrs. Lasseter was opening up her suitcase in my living room.

You never saw the beat of what she spread on my coffee table that day. And me fifty dollars poorer. I'm a sucker for those frosted bottles with sweet-sounding names. Banana cleanser and strawberry beauty mask and cucumber scrub. When this avocado gets soft, I could squeeze it and smear it on my nose. I don't think you ever completely get over it. Have you noticed how you can push your cart down the aisle, and your eyes stay on certain things? Look over there at the fruits and vegetables, all those greens and reds and yellows and oranges under the lights, those pink onions. You want to touch. That's the way it was. When she left, I sat on my sofa for a long time and unscrewed caps and rolled the frosted bottles against my face.

Mrs. Lasseter was a convincing lady. She made me believe I could sell that stuff to any and everybody. Before I knew what I was doing, I had settled down with the telephone book and looked up numbers and made a list. And went to Belk's shopping. They won't let you go out to sell unless you're in a dress and hose.

Then I was still working here and starting that, too. You'd come in here, and I'd be miles away figuring up in my head how much I'd ordered and thinking of one more name to add to my list. People would come through my line that I hadn't thought of yet, and I'd try to memorize their names until the line slowed down enough for me to get out a pad I kept under here on this shelf. Lottie Baynes, Lottie Baynes, I'd be thinking while I ran the cash register and pushed these items by. It would turn into a song in my head. Later, on my way across the parking lot in the dark, I'd still be singing it. Lottie Baynes, Agnes Haynes, Sue Belle Smith, and Trisha Grimes. I had it in my head I would call up those people and tell them I'd started selling "Esther's Real People" cosmetics, and they'd say hang on a minute and I'd hear them dropping all their Avon and Estee Lauder and Coty and K-Mart in the garbage clanging and rattling. That's how they do you. They make you think God is working it all out and changing people's minds. "Go chunk that Avon," he will say, and up they will go to sweep off the medicine cabinet shelves and make room for "Esther's Real People," which is more, you know, religious.

You should have seen Mrs. Lasseter when she came back from Omaha the first time. You'd have thought she'd seen God the way she was high as a kite. That's the way they do. It's like a Tupperware convention or a revival. You wave your hands up in the air and sing, and first thing you know, you're believing you can change the world, get everybody in Milledgeville, all shapes, sizes, colors, religious beliefs, and political parties, into "Esther's Real People."

How many babies you got now? You got somebody at home to help you carry all this food in? That's something that gets me. You have these high school boys here who won't even let you carry a little old sack with a grapefruit in it to the car, and you get home and carry eight or ten ten-pound bags from out at the road all the way up the steps by yourself. I guess doing it once beats twice though.

That first time Mrs. Lasseter came back from Omaha, she called a meeting of her girls out at the Days Inn. By the time she had fastened a pin on all of them and challenged them to go out and teach all manner of people how to do up their faces, I was convinced I was going to be one of her girls too. I hung around afterwards, and we went out to eat at the Golden Corral. I got out a piece of paper and asked her to tell me how to manage it. She told me exactly what to order and how much overhead I needed, and I took everything I had out of the bank and gave it to her. Come Monday, I went up there to Mr. Heal's office and told him I was quitting to take advantage of a once-in-a-lifetime opportunity.

Who's this cake for? Somebody got a birthday? Your oldest? Nine? Lord, Lord, time flies.

You think you got a load to carry. You should have seen the load on my front porch. When I got home, I liked to dropped dead.

What have I done? I said right out loud. There they were on my front porch, eight blue boxes with the silver letters "Esther's Real People" on the side, the boxes stacked like a pyramid from the biggest ones to the smallest ones, all shining in the sun.

Why didn't you get this bread sliced over there at the deli? It would be a lot easier for you with all those kids. You know they will want a piece on the way home, ball it up and suck on it. Least ways, that's what we used to do, unless video games have kids where they don't like to suck on bread anymore. It's done everything else.

Now listen at you, little boy. You let your mama talk to me. Those cartoons will be there when you get home. They aren't going anywhere.

Anyway, I carried those boxes in the house scared to death the sun had melted the lipsticks. Time I ripped open the boxes and lined everything up against the wall, I had twenty-five of everything. I worked all day making starter sets. In every box, I had one strawberry cleanser, one lemon astringent, one cucumber mask, and one night-time banana raindrops. On top of each box I put a complimentary powder mitt in the blue cellophane sack, an introductory offer. I love those powder mitts when I get out of the tub. Everything had a purpose. The cream base protector kept dirt and grime from getting in the pores. The mask tightened up the wrinkles. The night-time banana raindrops put the moisture back in.

Now, listen young man. Hard as your mother works, she doesn't have to listen to you whine. When I get through, I'll be through, and not a minute before. If you haven't learned patience before, then you can learn it now.

That's all right. Don't you apologize. I'm used to children. You ought to see some that come in here. I had to learn to be honest with them. Inside those little heads, children are adults like anybody. If you talk straight with them, they can understand. You mothers have to let me and the children handle it. Every now and then I have a mother to get mad, but not often. Those are usually the ones with the children who turn out to be juvenile delinquents.

Then I started calling the numbers on my list. The first time I did it, I sat there by the phone and couldn't get up my nerve. I had to call up Mrs. Lasseter to hear her tell me again that she thought I could. I won't call out the names here in the store, but out of ten names, six said yes and the other four hurt my feelings. You know, it's not easy to have somebody say no. I guess the hardest lesson I ever learned is that everybody has the right to say no. That's the gospel truth.

Each morning I got up at the same time to establish a routine. I'm a nine-to-five person. I put on my bow blouse and straight skirt and stockings and tailored jacket and my "Esther's Real People" stick pin right here. And I took my case with the kits and my Master Card imprinter—I liked to never learned how to use that joker--and I started my rounds. I don't know how the Avon ladies and the Jehovah's Witnesses stand it. At least I had my visits arranged and didn't have to be told no face-to-face. You can't hide your face, face-to-face.

We're not allowed to touch or do it ourselves. We tell others how and watch them do it. I sat there at many a kitchen table and watched transformations from a tired old housewife to a movie star. And you have to be a counselor too because they'll talk to you and tell you some things you wish they wouldn't. I know some things right now I wish I didn't. And people want things. They'd spend every dime they had.

Yes, for a while, I did like it, I'll have to tell you. If it was just that, visiting with people like that and making them look pretty and feel better that was all there was to it, I might have stayed in it. If that was all there was. But it was more.

You can't stay where you are in "Esther's Real People." You have to move up. You have to advance. Don't you think it's that way too much in this world? I knew one lady who was a nurse. She was the best nurse you ever saw, had the softest hands. When she'd wake you up in the middle of the night to check your blood pressure, you'd think an angel was standing by your bed. That was what she liked too, being with people. But first thing she knew, they had her stuck behind a desk filling out charts and checking on the other nurses.

That's the way they do. Before I knew it, Mrs. Lasseter was talking about going on an airplane to Omaha and getting diamond necklaces and maybe driving a silver Cadillac. It sounded like Raleigh coupons or Green Stamps or something. I don't know. One day I was feeling good like I was helping people, and the next day I felt funny. Shoot. I didn't even know where Omaha was.

That right? Well, not me. I never had been outside of Milledgeville. Didn't want to either. To me, running around all over creation means you aren't happy where you started out. I know a lady that fixes hair who takes off every chance she gets. First time I found that out, I said to myself, there's a lady looking for something. If you spend every cent you've got on an airplane, a boat, or a train, that tells me something right there about a person. But next thing I knew, I was sitting on a bus beside Mrs. Lasseter and had been up and down on an airplane.

Huh? Oh, it was all right for a one-time thing, but mostly I like to keep my feet on the ground. And the way people put it away on those planes, it's a wonder any of them know they've left the ground. I brought a cute bottle home to my nephew to show him what they looked like.

No, see it was the bus and not the airplane that turned out to be the problem. It wasn't supposed to be a bus. It was supposed to be a limousine. A special blue "Esther's Real People" limousine to pick us up. They promised.

Mrs. Lasseter looked fit to kill. If I could be that pretty at her age, I'm telling you, you couldn't tie me down. And when that limousine didn't come, I could have cried for her. On that bus, she kept her eyes closed the whole time and kept saying, "When we get there, I'm going to forget how we came." Like to tore me up.

Listen, Hilda, will you get this lady on your register? I'm not quite through here. Honey, move over and let Hilda get you. We got a few more here.

Don't worry, Hilda can handle it. Well, I'll make a long story short. You're going to have a lot of bags here. You see, there was this man. It was the pitifullest thing I about ever saw. I guess you only see it in big cities like that. But he was drunk or sick or something. I saw him asleep over there when we first got on, and I thought poor thing, ain't that pitiful, poor old black man. Mrs. Lasseter sat down and closed her eyes and waited.

We'd been about three blocks I guess when he pulled his old

gray head up and picked up this stick he had there on the seat. He held on to that metal bar and leaned over the bus driver's shoulder and shouted out, you couldn't hardly understand him, "Where I'm at? Where I'm at? Like that.

I'm ready, honey, you hold your horses. I don't see anybody having to wait, do you?

The bus driver said something like Fifth and Green, and the poor old thing mumbled under his breath, "I can't walk that far."

I knew then he'd slept through his stop, and I started wondering if he would have to ride back and forth, back and forth, and picturing in my mind what kind of place he must live in but never could imagine him having anything or ever being young or holding down a job or having a wife or anything. He looked scrubby and dirty and balled up there on the seat. I couldn't even imagine that seat without him in it. All of a sudden it seemed to me like that old buster had been riding that bus back and forth for centuries and asking where he was at and never one time being awake when it was his stop because he really didn't have a stop but just a bus to ride on.

As he settled back down in his seat, he looked over at us and hollered, "What time is it?"

I heard Mrs. Lasseter say, "Oh, Lord, how much farther?" and the next thing I knew the bus turned a corner real fast, and that poor old soul—I can't stand to think about it—he'd been sitting there pointing at us waiting for the time, and neither one of us had said anything. I didn't have on a watch. I had this Timex I wore out there, but Mrs. Lasseter told me it looked like a big old nurses' watch and didn't go with my evening dress, so I left it in the room. When the bus turned that corner, the man came up out of the seat and dived as straight into Mrs. Lasseter's lap as if he'd aimed. I'm coming. We're coming, for Pete's sake. It's not like I do this every day. And got grease and dirt off his face right in the middle of Mrs. Lasseter's dress.

She stood up and pushed the old thing out into the aisle, and he sort of moved back and forth on his hands and knees like a big baby or an animal, and I couldn't decide what to do. I was looking at Mrs. Lasseter's dress. I couldn't help feeling sorry for her. She was all dressed up and was supposed to go up on the stage and meet Esther and get an award, but now she had that man's face on the front of her dress.

I looked down at the man one time and somebody, I don't know who, said "He can get up by himself." So we pushed on past him to get off. The last I remember was him still on his hands and knees in the middle of the aisle and people pushing around him and stepping over him in a hurry not to miss their stop.

That was it for me. All through the program at the auditorium, all I could think about was his hands. Those fingers spread out and the people coming down the aisle with the big fat hateful shoes on their feet and probably not being careful and him helpless.

When I got back home, I saw all those boxes piled up. I had a special room I'd fixed to be my office and to keep my "Esther's Real People" supplies in. I walked in the door, put my suitcase down, and closed the door to that room. And for the life of me, I can't bring myself to go back in there. All that money tied up in boxes. Mrs. Lasseter's called me several times, and I always make up some excuse. I know I'll have to go in there sooner or later—all that stuff's got to be mailed back to the company—but I keep putting it off.

Listen, honey. Don't you ever let anybody tell you different. Peace right here in your heart is what matters. You save stamps? It's the only thing that matters. That comes to two hundred thirty-six dollars and nineteen cents. Things sure add up, don't they?

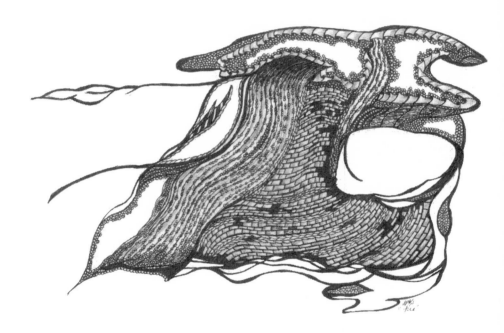

"Transients"

TRANSIENTS

"Whatsoever you do to the least of my people, that you do unto me."

--Matthew 25:41

Father Felix has gone to Australia to visit his brother who has cancer and may not live long. In his absence, Sister Kathaleen is holding a meeting of the Eucharistic Ministers. She stands at the front of the church wearing a red sweater-dress and boots. This is one of several meetings she intends to call while Father Felix is away. Next, she will assemble the lectors, the Parish Women, the choir, and the altar boys.

I will have to leave early tonight to go to an eight o'clock poetry reading at the college. It is now seven fifteen, and Sister is telling us that, as Eucharistic Ministers, we don't need to kneel at the altar during the Lamb of God. We are, at that point, she says, no longer lay people but extensions of the priest. Some of us have been kneeling, and it is distracting to the smoothness of the moment. Besides, she says, when some people get down, it is hard for them to get back up again.

"Any questions?" Sister Kathaleen asks.

Sheila Mayberry raises her hand and says, "What about genuflecting? Should we genuflect when we first go up to the altar?"

"Just bow," Sister says, and she turns and bends forward from the waist toward the Blessed Sacrament, to show how it is done. "All of this kneeling and genuflecting slows things down when it isn't necessary. Remember," she says, "the moment the Eucharistic Minister steps foot in the sanctuary at Mass, he becomes an extension of the Priest."

Looking at her watch and then back at the agenda, Sister moves on to the next item on her list. "There's to be a Synod on the laity," she says and begins passing out Xeroxed copies from a stack as big as the Sears catalog. "All the laity are to fill out these questionnaires and turn them in. Then we'll mail them to Atlanta where our responses will be put on the computer so our opinions can be made known at the

Synod. Remember this," says Sister, her index finger pointing straight up into the air. "There are only two things the priests can do that the laity cannot: hear confession and say Mass. The Church is not made up of only the Pope, the bishops, and the priests."

As she begins to pass out her Xeroxed copies, the back door to the church opens, and in step these two young fellows who look like those angels on "Highway to Heaven," sort of long-haired and whiskered and wearing blue-jean jackets. Sister thinks they're college boys looking for the fraternity meeting going on at the same time over in the parish hall, so she waves in that direction and says, "Over there." When they don't move, she says louder and points again, "The fraternity meeting is over there."

They still don't move but stand there with their hands in their pockets. All of us are turned around looking at them.

Sister sighs, puts down her Xeroxed copies, and walks back there to where they are. We sit and chat with one another while the three of them talk in the back of the church. When Sister comes back, she calls Jack out to the aisle to confer with him. "They are transients," she says to him. "They say they went to the police station, and the police told them to come over here. I swear I think there must be a mark out there on a tree. I guess Father has been standing at the door all this time handing out money to everybody who rings the bell."

"Well," says Jack, who is a Knight of Columbus and is supposed to be in charge of this sort of thing while Father is away, "I think Father knows which ones to give to and which ones to send on their way. I don't know one from the other, but I'll go talk to them."

While Jack stands in the back with the men, Sister announces that we will take a break until Jack gets the thing settled. As we wait, someone asks Sister about the car that caught on fire over at Cumming during the Civil Rights demonstration the other day, and we get off on that. She says it must have been a suicide, that the car was sitting off by the road in an abandoned place, and when the police found it, ten or twelve hours had passed. They couldn't even tell if the dead man was black or white. A priest who went over from Atlanta to march tried to anoint the body, but the police wouldn't let him.

Sister shrugs and says, "It would've been too late anyway.

Theology tells us that after one or two hours, the spirit leaves the body. One or two hours," she says, snapping her fingers, "and the spirit's gone."

"Twenty thousand people," someone says, "Can you believe it? I'll bet those Klansmen were surprised to see such a crowd."

"I saw on TV," Harriett Spillars says, "where one man was standing in the street and saw them coming, shaded his eyes, and said, 'God Almighty, look at them people!' This fat lady standing next to him said, 'Looks like they invading our town like a foreign army!'"

Jack comes back to the front of the church, and the door closes, the two young men gone. "They were painters," he says. "They travel around looking for jobs and hadn't had a job in two or three days. They drive a pick-up truck. I told them the priest was out of town, and we didn't know what to do."

Sister picks up her Xeroxed copies and starts to pass them out again. "The next thing I want this group to do," she says, "is to start carrying communion to the sick and the dying. We need to get into the nursing homes," she says.

When I have to leave to go to my poetry reading, I ask Jack to watch me walk to my car in case those men are still out there. One lady had her pocketbook snatched when she was leaving church a few weeks back, and it's got us all scared. As we open the door, Jack is saying, "Are they gone? Where could they have gone so soon? They said they hadn't eaten all day."

Behind us at the front of the church, Sister Kathaleen recites aloud her prayers, the ones she uses in the nursing home. She reads them to the older residents, she says, some of whom she is not even sure are Catholic. When some of the old people open their mouths to receive the host and she places it on their tongue, she says they spit it right back out again. You have to watch out for that, Sister says. If you don't mind, it will lie there on the front of their clothes. When the nurses come to take the tray, they'll think it's a piece of food.

"The Cows Chew Loud in Milledgeville"

THE COWS CHEW LOUD IN MILLEDGEVILLE

"Expectations are resentments under construction."

--Anne Lamott

In early November, after reading a spiteful, heartless and unChristian letter from her daughter-in-law, Sally B. Pierce dug up the Jerusalem artichokes from her garden. She only planted them because they looked pretty in the catalog. Now she didn't know what to do with them.

She wondered how she must look, squatting on the ground in the middle of her garden—her garden like a postage stamp—digging. Three cows strolled to the fence and stood chewing, chomping, watching.

No one could stare like a cow. The one on the left looked like Lottie Snied who phoned yesterday. "Hurry up, now, and come on back to church, Sally B. You get out of the habit, and you'll never be back."

Lottie had called to speak to her daughter Margaret and acted as though Sally B. couldn't hold a message in her head long enough to pass it on. "Tell Margaret," she had said, "tell Margaret that she's on the committee this month. The altar committee. She's to change the linen on the main altar and the two side ones. And ask her to see what she can do about the candle wax the altar boys dripped on the carpet. The altar linens. The candle wax. Okay? Okay?" Sally B. could have choked her.

The cow in the middle was her daughter-in-law the Snob who married her son Jackson and took him off to California and who had written Sally B. that awful letter which she wouldn't show to anyone not even Margaret and who wished Sally B. wouldn't ever open her mouth when they came home once every two years. Let her try to tell one thing.

"Did I ever tell you…" was all she said before that girl glanced at Jackson and they rolled their eyes, so obviously thinking together, Not this again.

It was either that sideways look between them or the polite

smile, the nod, the gaze which showed that Jackson had spoken with her ahead of time, and they had decided. She endured so patiently that when they got back home to California Jackson would give her roses for a reward. Unless, of course, Sally B. wrote him about the letter which she wasn't.

The third cow was someone Sally B. didn't know and, besides, she was tired of that game. Margaret would be home soon and they would have to eat fish. The Church changed but Margaret didn't. When you do something for years and years and build up a strong, healthy conscience, you can't start suddenly eating meat on Friday and feel good about it.

Margaret couldn't anyway. She wasn't built that way. Margaret was so Catholic that Sally B. believed if she had been born smack in the middle of a Pentecostal Holiness Independent Baptist revival in Waycross and the daughter of a visiting Preacher she would still have said Hail Mary before Mama.

But it wasn't Sally B.'s fault, and no letter would make her think it was. She would have raised the child Baptist if she could have figured out a way to do it. She became Catholic to marry the man she loved. Mr. Pierce's sisters, Margaret's Aunt Ann and Aunt Elizabeth, snatched Margaret up and whispered Catholic to her the instant she was born. Gave her rosaries and statues of the saints for her birthday instead of normal gifts. Had her baptized as a baby which was foolishness.

All those years of fish on Friday, and Sally B. never wanted any of it. When she became Catholic, she found a fairyland so full of saints like elves and nuns holding flowers that her head swam when she tried to pray. Who was the patron saint of Jerusalem artichokes? Of staring cows? Of seventy-five-year-old women with daughters who would rather have Holy Communion for supper than fried chicken?

Even Jesus separated into many figures that revolved around her head and wouldn't join into one point of light to pray to—Christ Crucified, the Sacred Heart, Jesus the Good Shepherd, Jesus in the Blessed Sacrament, the Holy Face, Jesus limp in the arms of His mother, the infant Jesus, the Body of Christ, the Blood of Christ—she wanted one. Only one. Like she had in the Baptist Church.

114

It was the Blessed Virgin's fault too, who had stepped in along with Ann and Elizabeth and took Margaret away from her at the beginning. The Virgin had always been Margaret's only mother, and Sally B. didn't think it was very Christian of her to do it.

So Margaret was peculiar. Her daughter-in-law thought she was telling Sally B. something she didn't already know. They lived together, didn't they, and them as different as night and day? Lord knows, she tried to make Margaret practical. To loosen up and have fun like other girls. To stop studying all the time. To think about something besides her students. To stay home instead of going to Mass every day. Hadn't she fixed supper exactly at 5:30 so Margaret would have to eat? Three people in Milledgeville must have gone to daily Mass and two of them Cubans. Margaret didn't have to be one.

Sally B.'s work in the garden was going well. The old staring cows could see that. The artichokes lay neatly in the dirt beside the rows of tomatoes. Her daughter-in-law thought she would read the letter, have a nervous breakdown, and go to the Milledgeville Old Folks Home. Sally B. told her the last time they were home that she wouldn't go to a nursing home as long as she could crawl over and drink water from the puppy's bowl.

Sally B. realized how stiff she had become as she stood, walked to the foot of the steps, and picked up the bucket that contained the torn letter. Swinging the pail by her side, she skipped to the fence and, leaning close to the middle cow, whispered, "Watch this, you old heifer."

Sitting on the ground beside the artichokes, Sally B. slid along the row and with a spoon dug twenty small holes. As she turned and moved back toward the cows, she reached into the bucket, dropped a piece of the letter into each hole, and covered it with dirt, patting the top of each tiny grave lightly with the back of the spoon.

Standing, she slung one artichoke at a time over the fence and into the cows' faces. The cows turned abruptly and ambled out to field, their tails swishing from side to side, knocking off flies.

Sally B. dragged the hose to the garden and sprayed a thin mist over the tomatoes, the beans, the squash, and the buried letter. Lifting the hose into the air, she watched a rainbow rise between her and the cows as the cool water washed her face. "In the name of the Father, and of the Son, and of the Holy Ghost. Amen."

When Margaret drove into the yard after Mass, Sally B. still watered the garden. The sun had settled behind the cows, throwing across the backyard a long, black shadow that fell into the birdbath and pointed at Sally B.

"Sam"

SAM

"You may be as different as the sun and the moon, but the same blood flows through both your bones. You need her, as she needs you."

--George R.R. Martin, *A Game of Thrones*

W hat do you think we should do with Sam?" Darlene asks, driving. She's got her hands up on top of the steering wheel, and I notice that her fingernails are painted a rust-color brown and she has on that gold filigree ring Daddy gave Mama and then Mama gave her. I have the black onyx one with the silver insignia that Mama gave Daddy, but I don't have it on. I don't wear rings much or paint my fingernails either. I cut them close because they get in my way when I try to pick up bobby pins, and sometimes that old purple rinse gets under them, and I have a terrible time getting it out. I have Mama's fingernails; Darlene has Daddy's, strong so they'll grow long like that.

We are on our way out to see our cousin Pam, who is peculiar. It's not Pam's fault, though. I blame Rebecca, Pam's mother, who was always jealous of Darlene, who is Pam's age and prettier and more popular than Pam. Rebecca acted as if she thought it was Mama's and Darlene's fault when Darlene won beauty contests and became a cheerleader. Darlene and Pam were never in the same group in high school, but still every time Darlene and Ed come home to Milledgeville from Tennessee, Darlene thinks she has to go out and see how Pam's doing.

"What do you think we should do with Sam?" Darlene asks again, talking louder and looking at me. She's referring to Mama's only doll, at home lying on his back among mothballs and blankets in the cedar chest. Sam is the only thing Mama can't figure out how to divide up when she passes away.

Darlene's talking about yesterday at lunch when we were all sitting around the table, Ed and Darlene on one side, me on the other by myself, and Mama at the head. We had finished eating (we had rice and stewed tomatoes--Darlene's favorite, Mama always has that when

119

they come home--fried chicken, creamed corn, and candied sweet potatoes for Ed--he could eat a whole platter by himself), and we had all put our cloth napkins up on the table and were sitting there talking. I stood up to go wash the dishes, and Mama raised her hand and closed her eyes with that look she gets and said, "No! We are not going to start cleaning up the kitchen. We are going to sit here and talk." Mama orchestrates every minute when Ed and Darlene are home so not one second will be wasted. She thinks I want to do the dishes to get out of talking.

The dining room is what got the conversation turned in that bent. It's like King Tut's tomb, containing all the things she wants to leave us, and Mama wants everything even. The table we all had our elbows on is going to me; it's paired up with the piano for Darlene. I'm supposed to get the hand-painted china, painted in a green crabapple design done by a woman Mama used to know who is dead now, and Darlene gets the silver.

But there's only one Sam, and Darlene and I both have sentimental feelings for that doll. In all her Christmases growing up, Mama only got this one doll, and we always knew he was lying in the cedar chest under blankets. As we were growing up, ever so often, maybe on a hot summer afternoon when there was nothing else to do, we said, "Mama, can we look at Sam?" and she went into the dining room and lifted out all the blankets and embroidered dish towels and tatting, and underneath would lie Sam with his brown head and long white gown. Darlene and I stood with our arms ready for a baby, and Mama laid Sam gently into first one and then the other's arms. I put my hand underneath the gown and felt his soft cloth body and his smooth brown feet with no shoes.

It was strange to us that Mama had only one doll. Every Christmas Darlene and I got a new one, so that by the time we were grown, we had a whole family. I've taken better care of my dolls than Darlene has. All my dolls are in my house, lined up on the bed in the guestroom. I'm not sure Darlene even knows where hers are, so I say, "We could let the Family and Children's Services decide which one of us is more deserving."

"I've taken care of my dolls," Darlene says, right off, "and I don't appreciate you always acting like I've let them go downhill. My dolls are in as good a shape as yours are."

Darlene has been taking therapy and has been practicing speaking her piece. Several times since she and Ed came home, she has stood in the floor and shaken her finger at us, telling us what she thought. Her therapist told her she ought to practice being assertive, and since she explained that to us, Mama acts like it's all right for Darlene to say whatever she wants. Mama wants Darlene and me to be close so we can look after one another when she's gone. She tries to arrange times for us to be alone, like this trip out to Pam's. She wouldn't come with us but said, "You girls need some time to yourselves." Then when we get home, she grills us about what we talked about.

So I say, "Where are your dolls right now? Tell me where they are."

"You don't know everything about me," Darlene says. "There are a lot of things you don't know."

When I think back to Darlene and me, how we were growing up, I can't remember that much about her on a day-to-day basis, and I wonder if I ignored her. What I remember are traumatic experiences, like the Mother's Day she forgot a gift and I gave her one of mine. I remember how Mama made a big to-do over that bath powder I let Darlene give her, more than my earbobs. And I remember those words coming out of my mouth, almost against my will, "I bought both presents, Darlene forgot," and being so sorry the minute I said it because I saw Darlene's red cheeks and her lip began to tremble and those big fat tears start to roll down her face. It was like I was a horrible person that God had turned against, and I didn't think I would ever be able to think of myself as a good person again. Later I was lying across my bed sobbing, and though Mama sat down beside me--I felt the bed go down--and began rubbing my back in circles, around and around, I couldn't believe I was forgiven.

Then one Christmas Darlene did something to me that I won't forget. Since I was the oldest, I was the one who always went to the living room first to see what Santa Claus brought. I walked down the hall in the dark, the leader, Darlene holding onto my pajama top behind me. I reached up and flipped on the light, and we saw our new dolls together, hers in the chair on the right, mine on the left. We ran to them, picked them up, and held them to us--that wonderful smell of a new doll's face. But that one Christmas we were there, holding our dolls, and something about the way Darlene looked at mine, something about her voice when she said, "Aren't they pretty?" made me know at that moment that she had already been to the living room early without me, while I was still asleep. She had seen my doll before me and spoiled my Christmas morning.

It was times like these that made Darlene and me find it hard to look one another in the eye.

"We could cut him in half like King Solomon," I say.

"Ha, ha," says Darlene. "It is impossible to carry on a serious conversation with you."

There are things about me that Darlene doesn't know, too. She thinks she knows me, but she doesn't know me completely. For example, she doesn't know that I've been drunk before. And she doesn't know that I've slept with two different men. And she doesn't know that I even had sex with a girl one time.

I'm embarrassed about it, and I try not to tell many people. I've told two so far. It was sort of weird, like sleeping with yourself, and I learned how to sleep with myself a lot better after that. But now it's my big secret that I feel changed me in some way and made me a different person. So when I think of the secrets I have that Darlene doesn't know, that's the big one.

I've tried to imagine how it would be to tell her, and I always feel that one day I will, one day when our five years apart seems narrower. At times I think it would be so easy. In my mind I picture the two of us sitting like any two sisters you might see on television talking, and I see my mouth moving, me telling her and her listening and then us both crying and putting our arms around each other. When I picture it, we're all in a haze sitting on a brick wall somewhere with a flower garden below, and it's all beautiful and simple like those Kotex commercials on television.

Sometimes I can understand how easy it could happen, and it seems like I could say it so that other people could understand it too, especially my own sister. I think Darlene could understand about

Stella. Maybe I'll even tell her today on the way home from Pam's riding in the car. I'll say, "Darlene, I have something I'd like to tell you, something that was important in my life, and I've decided I'd like to share this with you."

Then I'll tell her. She already knows Stella. At least she's met her once when she and Ed came into the shop when they were home last year. We had fixed the shop up with a new sign out front that said "Hair Port" and then "unisex" written underneath it in smaller letters. Some days we have more men than women. There are six chairs in our shop, but all of us don't work every day. We stagger it so there will always be somebody working every day except Sunday.

The shop belongs to Mary Dunlap, and her chair is down at the front as you come in the door. That way she can hear everything the receptionist, Hilma, says when she answers the telephone. Mary doesn't let much of anything slip by her in the shop, but she doesn't know much about our private lives. As far as I know, she never got a hint about what happened with Stella and me.

Then after Mary is Alice, who cuts mostly teenagers' hair. She's got her hair dyed black and shaved over one ear and the top sticks straight up. When she fixes it, she puts heavy gel all over the top in a glob and then pulls it straight up with a comb. Stella and I look at one another and roll our eyes, but when we talk seriously about it, we are really glad because our shop needs to keep up with the times and provide something for everybody. Alice wears something different every day; for example, right now as I'm thinking of her, I'm picturing her with high-heeled pointed-toed shoes and textured old-timey black hose with seams up the back. And a skirt so short she couldn't stoop down to pick up a curler without taking somebody's picture. Alice is still young now, but she won't be able to work at this job long and still wear those heels and hose. Your feet and legs give out soon enough even when you wear Hushpuppies or those SAS nurses' shoes with the good arch supports.

Then there is Kitty, who cuts a bit of everything and Ida Mae, who does mostly older men. Stella and I are down at the far end, first Stella and then me. I like being at the end with a wall beside me. Even in church I like to go to the end of the pew so I have people on one side of me and not both. I have a sign over my corner with my name on it, and a plaque with a saying that I like, "Desiderata." It says what I believe, and sometimes when someone is telling me this long story about her life, I will look over there at that poster, and I don't even have to read it. I look at it, and it reminds me what I believe.

Stella will be over there talking up a storm. She does a lot of old ladies. She has a way with them. She's got a good sense of humor and is married to a black man, but Mary doesn't know that. All day Stella and I stand there and carry on conversations in the mirrors in front of us so that at the end of the day when we are putting on our coats and look at each other face to face without the customers there, it seems unnatural, as if we have turned into one another.

Stella has reddish brown hair, which always looks fried on the ends. "I have such awful hair," she's always saying to her customers, and while each of her customers has to hear that once, I have to hear it about a dozen times a day. She has a turned up nose, and her lips are always red because she chews on them.

Stella is a happy-go-lucky person who always does what she wants to do at the moment without questioning herself. She never pays attention to what the rest of the world is doing. But I do care. I compare myself to other people and wonder if because I went along with Stella that night if it brands me for life. Stella doesn't think so. She thinks every experience a woman has in life makes her a better person. But I think we all have these tapes inside. And anything we put on our tape can automatically cut on and start playing out for the entire world to hear. Some things on our tapes get buried and stay buried for years and years, and then one day we get in a nursing home, and all our relatives wonder where in the world we learned that.

This is an example of how Stella is so spontaneous. One day in our shop we were all standing there and in walked a homeless-looking man who told us to give him everything out of the cash register. His hand was covered with a brown paper sack, and he was pointing it at us like it was a gun. Stella took the bobby pins out of her mouth and said to the robber in a soft, understanding voice, "Now what would your Mama say if she saw you stealing? I don't believe I could stand it if I stole something." And then she looked at my reflection in the mirror and said, "Could you? Could you stand to spend stolen money? I think it would burn my pocket clean through."

That robber stuffed his pockets with every bit of the money out of the cash register and left the shop without ever saying a word. I could tell it hurt Stella's feelings.

That's the way things happened with Stella and me. She does what she feels at the moment, and that night, what she felt like doing was kissing me. She had a customer earlier in the day, a pretty girl with long, shiny hair. When the girl left, there weren't any customers in the shop at the moment, and Alice called over to Stella's chair, "You know she's funny, don't you?"

"No, honey, that the truth?" Stella said. Alice started to tell Stella about how she heard it, and Stella said to herself and to me, "She sure doesn't look it."

Later that day Stella and I were staying late in the shop to do one another's hair. I'd already done hers, and it looked good. I did it like a pageboy, and the ends were turning under, smooth and even. I sat in the chair while she did me a style we picked out of Hairdo magazine where the hair swoops back over one ear and hangs loose over the other. Stella had given me a shampoo, and I was feeling woozy and limp, like I get when somebody messes with my hair. "I can hardly walk," I said, as I stood with a white towel over my head and started back to the chair. Stella laughed and started combing out my wet hair.

"I wish I had nice hair like this," she said softly. I heard her voice as from the end of a tunnel as she ran the comb through my hair, and then she said, "I never would have thought that girl was funny."

I don't think I answered her, and she got the hair dryer and started blowing my hair and curling it around the brush. Then I heard her say, "I wonder what it's like?" and she kept fooling with my hair. I sat there with my eyes closed.

Then I heard her turn the hair dryer off and lay it on the counter, and she started fixing my hair with her fingers, curling the left side around my ear and shaping the right into a wave. I felt her lean down close to me from behind and put her head next to mine, her cheek next to my face. "You want to try it?" she said, and when I opened my eyes and looked in the mirror at her, she was smiling this nice easy way, her eyes quiet, and I could see that she was dead serious. She'd been thinking about that girl all day and had got her curiosity all worked up.

Any other time I might have been shocked or gotten mad, but I was so comfortable sitting there with her doing my hair that when she took my hand and led me to the back room to the flowered cot we keep back there, I followed her with the pink plastic cape still tied around my shoulders.

It was pretty exciting, too. Thinking back on it now, I'm glad it happened. Those big soft lips of hers were wet, and her body was warm and round, her face soft against mine, her clean newly-fixed hair smelling so good. There's something about the way one woman's face feels against another's, that's the thing I remember noticing first. We took off all our clothes, and I couldn't believe the sensation, like being all rolled up in your own body, like being completely yourself, more yourself than you've ever been before, like double yourself and more completely feminine, the complete girlness of being a woman, sweet and pink and soft and that ripeness of pure sex all over the room. We stayed there for a long time, and I remember wanting to stay, not wanting to move on to whatever came next.

"It was nice, wasn't it?" Stella said. "Different and nice." She sat up and looked down at me. "I mean, I can see how people might like it."

"You're a crazy girl," I said, but it was like everything was changed. I could see into the next day and knew that Stella and I would have a hard time looking at one another in the mirror again.

"Don't tell Henry, okay?" I said.

"Are you crazy?" she said. "He'd have a fit. He'd think it was a reflection on him."

Then there was that old flighty Stella, putting on her clothes and her mind already on Henry and what he was doing at home.

In the parking lot beside our cars, she kissed me one more time, long and soft, and said, "I'm glad we did it," then from her car window, "Men are still best, though, right?" And I was surprised after she drove off that I felt hurt, as if I'd been rejected.

Darlene is pulling into Pam's front yard, and she laughs, pointing at a sign over the garage that says, "Never mind the dog. Beware of the owner." My heart's beating real fast because I'd been imagining how I would tell Darlene, and I was getting scared thinking about it.

Pam answers the door wearing short shorts that look too tight in the crotch, and she has a cigarette in her hand. She doesn't smile but says, "Hey, come on in," real matter-of-factly.

We go in and sit down on a fluffy-looking velour sofa in shades of gold and brown with a glass-topped table in front of it trimmed in brass. All of this is probably still sitting on a credit card and not paid for. That's the way Pam's mother did too, except she ran up bills on clothes. As Pam and Darlene go over to the two chairs across from me, I notice that Pam is as straight as a beanpole and doesn't have any curves at all. She's one of those people who goes into a clothing store and finds out that all the clothes look better hanging on the hanger than on their own body.

Pam and Darlene sit down and start talking fast to each other, catching up. The first thing I see are some Playgirl magazines lying on the coffee table. Darlene picks one up and says, "Oh, neat! I wish I could subscribe to these, but Ed would have a fit." Then she looks over at me and says, "Have you ever seen one of these?" Sometimes Darlene treats me like I'm a missionary from China. I say no I haven't and she says, "Well, here, look! It's part of your education! If you've never seen one, you should."

I feel embarrassed to look, with both of them sitting there looking at me, so I say, "I will in a minute. You two go ahead and talk. I want to look out the window at your backyard, Pam," and I start getting up.

"Oh, it looks awful," Pam says. "I haven't cut the grass in two weeks, and the weeds are taking over."

I walk over to the dining room and look out the window at the yard. It's a plain old yard with grass and two trees and a chain link fence, no flowers or anything. I hear Pam and Darlene start to talk. Pam is telling Darlene that she has started dating a new boy who is the assistant manager at the Piggly Wiggly. She is telling her that he has long black hair around his shoulders and looks like a hippy.

When I sit back down and pick up one of those magazines, Pam and Darlene don't stop talking and don't seem to notice me. I start flipping through the pages. I've never seen anything like this before. I can't believe something like this could actually be published. It seems like it would be against the law, but here it is, a subscription coming to my cousin's house once a month and lying on her coffee table in plain view for the pest control man or anybody to see. I've only actually seen two men in my life without their clothes on; one, Milton Brown in high school who's the boy I dated the longest, and the other, Harrison Hartley, whose hair I cut for a year before we broke up and he started going to a regular barber. In those cases, you don't really see them, I mean out like this so that you can look at them. That's one reason I was glad Harrison and I broke up, because he used to want to turn on the light and look at me, you know, down there, and I used to be scared he was a pervert or something.

But these men in this magazine are there, facing the camera and not trying to hide anything. Their parts are showing, pages and pages of them, and all of a sudden I'm wishing I could get off by myself away from Pam and Darlene and really look at them. I'm trying to look casual, flipping the pages, and I'm hoping Pam and Darlene aren't paying any attention to me. Darlene is telling Pam something about Ed's job as a plant manager, gesturing real big and making it sound funny. Every now and then Pam will laugh, and I look to be sure they haven't noticed me.

Every one of these men is gorgeous, from head to toe, and their skin is such a perfect smooth color, so even, their bodies filled out and muscular. Some of them have black hair over their chest and others have a thin streak of hair up the middle. But it's hard to look only at their faces and shoulders and chests, and I find that my eyes keep moving down to their parts. It's like somebody has tapped me on the shoulder and showed me an animal inside of me, and I say, Oh! So there it is! Deep inside I can feel one of those low wicked sounds a cat makes.

Then I turn the page, and I can't believe what I see. It's a black man, as dark as an Ethiopian. He's standing there tall and naked, turned slightly to the side with one leg propped up on a stool and brown leather thongs on his feet. And over his shoulder he has a denim jacket trimmed in leather, holding it there with his fingers in a casual, macho way.

Then I let myself look at his parts. And as I look, I think of Stella and Henry, whom I have never seen, and of her white freckled body up close to his black skin, pushed tight, as close as any two can be, and I'm not thinking any words but feeling quiet inside as I think of them. It is like for the first time I can see in my mind a picture of them together, touching. It is a picture I want to sit and listen to and watch until I get used to it.

Then I hear Darlene and Pam talking to me. Pam is saying she wonders where they get those men, they sure aren't from around Milledgeville. I close the magazine and put it down on the table, and Pam asks if we want a coke. Darlene says she'll help her, and when the two of them go into the kitchen, I pick up the magazine again.

Their voices get low, and I'm looking at this red-headed man when I hear Darlene say, "I never thought I'd take off all my clothes in front of other women's husbands before, but it didn't seem all that strange."

"What did you say?" Pam asks. "Skinny dipping at the lake with other couples?"

I put the magazine down and cover my ears with my hands. In my mind I am picturing my sister Darlene, whom I watched turn into a young woman, developing breasts and pubic hair, being embarrassed if I walked into the bathroom as she was taking a bath, that Darlene whose body I know so well, almost as well as I know my own, taking off her clothes and walking out on a dock and other people looking at her. In my mind I want to run out there and throw a towel over her and tell her not to ever tell Mama or even more, not ever to tell me.

On the way home Darlene wants to ride by the cemetery to visit Daddy's grave. As she drives, I'm looking out the window at the houses passing by, and I'm thinking about how in each of those houses there are mamas wiping their hands on their aprons and children growing up and things family members could tell their friends but ought not ever tell each other.

When Darlene stops the car, I open my door and get out before she even gets the ignition turned off. By the time she has pulled up the brake and locked the doors, I am already standing beside Daddy's grave.

A huge ant bed is lapping over the top half of Daddy's gravestone, covering up his first name and his birthdate, leaving only the date of his death and our last name. Darlene comes up behind me and says, "I'm glad Mama's not here to see this."

She goes to the edge of the woods and finds two sticks, gives one to me, and begins tearing into the ant bed. I stoop down to help her, my stick breaks, and I stand up and begin kicking at the red dirt with my foot. The ants are running everywhere, and we keep poking and backing off, again and again. We have unearthed hundreds of paths leading in every direction, intersecting one another, branching off, running parallel, and all the ants are moving frantically, the sunlight having been let into all of their secret places. Finally we have the ant bed leveled, and Darlene finds a spigot sticking out of the ground on a lot near ours and fills up an old coke bottle. She pours water on the gravestone, and with our hands, we smooth the water off and clean out the letters of Daddy's name. Then we stand side by side and look at what we have done.

There are five graves across the lot--Daddy's mother and father, then Daddy with a space beside him for Mama, and then Daddy's two sisters on the other side.

"Where will you be buried?" Darlene asks, looking at me. Darlene will be buried in Tennessee with Ed and his family. I look at Mama's spot and Daddy's mother and wonder where the rest of their family is, the mother's side that gets lost, the woman's whole background, even her name, lost with each generation.

"It's going to be a tight fit," I say, "but I think there's room down here next to Aunt Mabel. I told Mama there was plenty of room for me turned sideways at everybody's feet, but she told me they don't allow you to be turned sideways." Here, mama had told me, meaning the cemetery, everybody has to be facing in the same direction.

"You're crazy," says Darlene, squeezing my shoulder, and I turn and start walking up the hill to the car. Directly in front of me in the distance is the tall steeple of the Baptist church where both Darlene and I were baptized. I get in the car and close the door, and then Darlene gets in. She cranks the car and says, "Let's don't tell Mama about the ant bed, okay?"

Before I know what is happening, I'm crying big sobs, my face in my hands. It feels as if I haven't cried like this in a long time, in years and years, maybe since I was a girl. Darlene turns off the car and puts her hand on my back and pats. "What is it, Honey?" she asks, but all I can do is shake my head.

When we get home, Ed and Mama are sitting in the living room talking. Ed is in the recliner with a Lewis Grizzard book lying on the table beside him. The title is *When my Love Returns from the Ladies' Room, Will I Be too Old to Care?* Mama has on her apron and is rocking back and forth in the chair, her bedroom shoes tapping the floor.

"I've decided what we could do with Sam," I say, walking in.

"What?" asks Mama.

"We could have joint custody. Darlene could keep him a year, and I could keep him a year. Every Christmas we could wrap him up like a present, and give him back to one another."

"Sounds like living out of a suitcase to me," says Mama, and Darlene and I look at one another, straight in the eye.

"The Vacuum Cleaner"

THE VACUUM CLEANER

"Nothing sucks like an Electrolux."

--1950's Swedish advertisement.

The Electrolux salesman looked like a preacher, black suit with white shirt, black tie. I was sitting on the floor coloring in a Lennon sisters coloring book. As I outlined Janet's Mary Jane shoe in burnt sienna, the man leaned forward to touch the machine sitting on the green carpet and said, "The Electrolux is the Bible of vacuum cleaners."

Annie was padding around on her little brown feet, dusting the new black-and-white television set. When the preacher took out a flat-ended piece, inserted it into the light gray hose, and turned on the Electrolux, the Bible roared to life, and the man began to vacuum the draperies, which pulled outward as if the tool was going to suck them up. Annie stopped and watched, her mouth open, the dust rag in her brown hand.

§

My mother couldn't believe that she had French doors, a big dining room with a shiny hardwood floor, and a maid. All she knew before she married my daddy was poorness. Poor sharecropping father, a different cold house every year, picking cotton, sleeping six to a bed, turned around sideways, a hot brick from the fireplace heating up the bed before they lined up. I imagined my mother's brothers and sisters as children lined up across the one bed like sardines in a can. Daddy's family came from poorness too. Daddy was a hard-working barber who saved every penny and made it possible for Mama even to consider buying a fancy electric machine that could sweep the floor and clean the curtains.

After the salesman left that day, Mama let Annie try out the new machine. Soon Annie was dragging that machine behind her all over the house, over the green carpet in the living room and down the hardwood floors in the shiny hallway and in the bedrooms.

§

133

Mama didn't ask Daddy for a maid until after I was born. Having to iron those ruffles on my Sunday School dresses made her feel as if she was being punished for something. Sallie was my best friend who lived down the street, and her mother had a maid, so after much pleading and pouting and giving Daddy the silent treatment, Mama hired the same maid that Sallie's Mama had. Sallie's family had gotten a TV before we did as well, and when Sallie's Mama brought Sallie's clothes up to the house for me to wear, Mama accepted, even though Sallie was bigger than I, and even though Sallie told everybody at school that I had on her old skirt.

§

The first day that Annie came to work, her son Arthur pulled up in the driveway in a beat-up car, navy blue with the paint coming off the sides, as if the car had tried to squeeze through a too narrow space. Annie shut the car door behind her and walked down the side of the house and around to the back door, up the steps, and rapped lightly on the screen. Mama let her in and showed her a nail beside the back door where she could hang her sweater. Automatically, Annie took off her shoes and padded barefooted into the kitchen. It was as if there were a manual that existed entitled, "Rules for Being a Maid:" 1. Go around to the back door; 2. Hang your coat on a nail; and 3. Take off your shoes.

Annie knew how to iron. She stood at the ironing board, the steam rising, while my colored dresses lined up on the rack beside her, no wrinkles anywhere, and starched so stiff they could stand up by themselves. Annie smelled like wood smoke. It was a smell that I associated with all colored people. I thought they smelled different from white people. It was only much later in my life that I learned that the smell came from the wood they burned in their fireplaces to heat their houses. I also learned that it was bad manners to call them "Nigra"; instead, "Colored People" was the nice and proper term. We didn't have a fireplace, but a gas heater bordered with a brick mantel where we hung our Christmas stockings. When the heater was turned low, the flame burned like a row of blue teeth.

Annie was short and small, and she hummed to herself as she ironed. She was about the same age as Mama. She liked hot Coca-colas in the green glass bottle, soft peppermint, and cake with chocolate inside and out. For Christmas from Mama she wanted big-legged bloomers from Roses Ten Cent Store and peach snuff in a can from the Little Star grocery store. After Christmas, she told Mama that Sallie's mother had given her a long list of gifts, not just the two that Mama gave. She wanted her families to save all their newspapers so that she could take them home to put up over her windows and walls to keep her house warm in the winter and cool in the summer.

§

One day when I was lying on the floor reading near the ironing board, I asked Annie, "What does m-i-r-r-o-r spell?"

Annie laughed, not answering, not telling me the word, her peach snuff tucked in her protruding bottom lip.

I got exasperated, and I raised my voice. "Tell me! I really need to know!" I said. "Ma-ma! Make Annie tell me what this word spells!" I tried to imagine Annie's house with the newspapers stuck up on the walls, all those words surrounding her. She should tell me what a word spelled. Mama told me after Annie left that day that I didn't have to say "Yes Ma'am" to Annie. I didn't understand because Annie was my elder, like Sallie's Mama, and I had to say "Yes Ma'am" to her. What was the difference?

§

Annie knew how to play with me. I sat in a red wagon, waiting for Annie to pull me around the yard. The wagon fit me, my butt at one end and my heels at the other. Dragging the wagon, Annie bumped me in circles under the pecan trees and ran me fast down the hill that separated the upper yard from the lower. When I stocked the shelves of the outside playhouse with empty Sweetheart Soap boxes or empty cans of pork and beans, Annie came to buy from me. When I played cooking, taking the seed pods off the mimosa trees and putting them in a metal pan with a handle, or mixing mud and water for chocolate pudding, Annie came to pretend eat. "I'll have me some of them collard greens," she said, looking down at the bowl of crushed clover and water.

I put my Mr. Potato Head game away with the Irish potato still in the box, punctured with holes from the plastic nose and ears and big lips. The box filled with long white sprouts, and months later when I pulled it out to play, Annie heard me scream all the way over the vacuum cleaner in the living room.

§

When I was a teenager, my boyfriend Tommy gave me a white bunny for Easter; the bunny grew into a big boy rabbit named Tommy that sprayed pee on anybody who came to feed him. Mama gave the rabbit to Annie, and when I asked her, "How's Tommy?" she answered, "Oh, he's hopping around in the yard with the chickens." It was only years later that I realized that Tommy probably got eaten the day she took him home.

Anything Mama got rid of, Annie took. If she didn't need it herself, she said she knew someone who did. One time when I went with Mama to Annie's house in the Bottom, I saw the old lamp from our living room, the picture of Jesus, the old holey throw rug, and the blue vase. Except for the newspaper wallpaper, Annie's house looked like a miniature version of our own.

When my daddy died too young, at age fifty-seven, Annie came over and padded silently among the crowds of people, washing dishes, picking up glasses, cleaning and straightening. She stayed at the house during the funeral to make sure we weren't robbed by someone who read the obituaries looking for an opportunity to rob a house that had French doors and a nice dining room. She had dinner ready when the family all got back to the house, and when the house was quiet again, everybody having left, she said to Mama, "The Lord move in mischievous ways."

When Annie's own husband died, a man she called Mr. Marshall, Annie simply came to work, said, "Mr. Marshall passed," and continued to clean. Later when she had a new man, a Mr. Hightower, she said she wasn't going to get married again. "I've done changed my name once. I ain't gone do it again."

§

Annie could interpret dreams. When I had a strange dream, I held it in my head until Annie came so that I could tell it to her. If you told a dream before breakfast, it would come true, so if it was a bad dream, I wouldn't tell Annie my dream until after I had eaten my breakfast. If it was something good, I told Annie before breakfast, just in case.

When in the tenth grade I cheated in my history class, I got down on my knees at night and promised God that I would quit, as soon as that course was over, and never cheat again. Then that night I dreamed I was all alone in an airplane, and the plane had no steering wheel or controls. "It was really scary," I told Annie. "The plane was turning and twisting and diving, and I couldn't do anything." Standing in the kitchen, I waved my arms in the air to show Annie how the airplane went. "What does it mean?" I asked.

"It mean you trapped and somebody else telling you what to do," Annie said.

"What did you dream last night?" I asked Annie. When Annie dreamed about horses, that meant somebody was going to die. It happened when Mr. Marshall died. He was perfectly fine, but one night Annie dreamed about lean hungry horses in the cemetery, walking among the graves, and then one white horse sprouted wings and flew up to Heaven. The next day Mr. Marshall had a heart attack and died right on his front porch. Annie had her dream too the night before my daddy died. That time the horses were walking around as always, their heads hanging down, their rib cages shining white in the dark. Suddenly, one horse tripped and fell into an open grave, Annie heard one whinny, and the horse was gone.

§

Mama told me never to tell secrets to my friends. "They will tell," she said, "and you'll be sorry you told."

But Mama and I both told Annie things. As Annie stood on the back screened-in porch ironing, the cord plugged into the socket of the swinging bulb over her head, Mama stood nearby, her arms folded across her chest. When I was a rebellious teenager, Mama told Annie about how sassy I was and how I hurt her with my disrespectful ways.

"She's so hurtful sometimes," said Mama. She sounds like she hates me."

"She don't hate you," said Annie. "She growing up."

"If her daddy was here, he would never let her talk to me like that," said Mama. "I've cried until I can't cry any more."

"Tears be the Lord's way to empty out our hurts," said Annie.

When I got put on social probation my freshman year in

137

college for drinking in the dorm, Mama didn't tell any of her church friends or neighbors or family members. She told Annie. Sitting at the breakfast table drinking instant coffee, Annie drinking a hot coca-cola out of the bottle, Mama said, "My daughter has done the one thing that would have broken her father's heart. His brother was bad to drink and wrecked his whole family's life. I'm so glad her daddy's not here to see this."

Annie sat and listened, her dark eyes watery in her shiny black face, her tiny braids sticking out from under her head wrap, and said, "Sometimes it be like that. The Lord make all things right in his time."

I didn't follow my mother's advice about talking to my friends. I told Amy when I first had sex with my boyfriend. And I told Barbara when I got caught drinking in the dorm. But I didn't tell them everything. Some things, I could only tell Annie.

"Daddy was my buddy," I told her. "I don't like for Mama to talk to me about Daddy. He was mine." I told Annie when my heart broke when my seventh-grade teacher, Miss Hendricks, moved away and how I kept having dreams about her for years.

Sometimes Annie didn't know what to say, so she listened. "The Lord make all things clear," she said, or "You smart. You got the good understanding."

§

Later as a teacher, I learned how to teach young black males. I stood at the door of my classroom as they came in, walking down the hall toward me, their legs moving in that familiar swagger, their full lips spread into broad, white-toothed smiles. I loved the way, at the first of the semester, they came into my room, and I could see it on their faces, another old white lady. Their faces sulky, their long-legged bodies slunk down into their desks, looking up at me with those eyes that could be filled with hatred but that I knew showed distrust and caution. I began silently, on the right side of the room, holding my hand out to the first student sitting there, taking his big rough hand into mine, holding it until our eyes met, until his face softened, until he smiled, laughed nervously, gave me a thumbs up. Moving slowly, I went to the next student, taking the hand, holding it. As I moved around the room, the snickering began. This lady was crazy. They were intrigued.

And then there was Rodney in my class. Annie's grandson. I remembered him as a boy, sometimes coming in to pick up a box of newspapers or some hand-me-down clothes. I had seen him running around the pecan trees in our yard, his energy propelling him in huge circles, faster and faster.

The ninth grade Rodney in my class was a handsome young man, shiny caramel skin, high cheekbones and wide-set eyes. In class he was quiet, and when I shook his hand, his eyes said, Don't let on you know me.

The writing activity was a childhood memory story. Rodney's paper showed talent, an ability to choose the right detail. He wrote of a dog he had and of living with his grandmother. He wrote of the next-door neighbor, whose wig was half on, half off, showing bits of lint from the side. His grandmother, he wrote, made chocolate chip cookies for him. He played with his dog in the yard. He named his dog Killer. One day, he wrote, Killer ran into the street and got hit by a bronze Lincoln Continental. The boy Rodney ran crying to his grandmother, and together they watched out the window as the big trash truck came by and scooped up Killer, threw him in the back, and drove off.

Another story Rodney wrote was about his church. He was the youngest child to say his Easter speech. He toddled to the front of the church and stood in the middle, looking around with his wide frightened eyes, not saying anything for a full two minutes, while the people on the front row nodded in encouragement. Then he spoke, firmly and distinctly, "Easter here, Easter there, Easter Easter everywhere."

Another time Rodney was sitting in church, holding his two dimes and a nickel, tied tightly in a white handkerchief, the way Annie had fixed it for him. He was going to keep his money and go to the store after church to get himself a soda. But his grandmother could read his mind. Suddenly he saw her navy-blue pointed-toed shoes standing there in the aisle beside his chair. The offering plate was being passed. Tighter and tighter he squeezed the knotted handkerchief in his fist, until his knuckles turned white. His grandmother reached down and pried his fingers loose, one by one, peeled the handkerchief free, unknotted it, and put the money back into his palm. "Now," she said, and he dropped the money into the plate as it passed.

I taught my students to help one another with their writing in helping circles. Rodney became the leader, and he was fascinated with revision, how adding more detail could make his story better. One day I looked up during my sixth period Advanced Senior English class, and there sat ninth grader Rodney, having snuck out of his science class to listen in.

Rodney won the Celebration of Writing award for the entire ninth grade and was given a plaque at the school board meeting. Sitting in the front row was Annie, her face proud. The school superintendent took a photograph of the three of us, Annie, Rodney and me—standing in the front of the room beside the American flag.

§

The neighborhood where Annie lived was called The Bottom because it was at the foot of a long hill and was one of the lowest places in town. The unpaved dirt street was composed of a row of houses beside the river. All the houses were unpainted, the wood weathered, and the yards filled with colorful flowers. It was a close-knit neighborhood where the women raised their children and grands, and people sat on the porches until long past dark.

Every year in the middle of the summer, they held the Bottom Reunion, and many of the older residents who had moved away came home for the weekend. There was a big barbeque, gospel music in the streets, and a long table spread with food. The old people sat on the porches, and the young people gathered in the streets. The newspaper sent a reporter to write about the reunion of the old neighborhood.

When it happened, Annie was walking down the alley from her house, dragging a folding chair behind her with one hand, and cradling a large plastic bowl of potato salad in the crook of her arm. Across the street she saw Rodney, his hand waving in the air, his gold teeth flashing, and him running toward her across the street.

She never really heard the sound. All she remembered later was his body arching backwards, falling into the dirt, and jerking until it became still. The first sound Annie heard was her own voice wailing, her mouth in an O, and seeing her potato salad turned upside down in the dirt.

When I went to the black funeral home to view Rodney and sign the book, the funeral home director treated me as if I were Mother Teresa. He bowed from the waist and said, "Yes, Ma'am" to me, even though he was much older than I.

Rodney's face had that white dusty look that my students called "ashy." In the Winter I had seen them passing a bottle of Jergen's lotion around the room. "My arm ashy" a student would say, in defensive explanation when I complained.

"Hey, Bro, yo face ashy," one of his friends might have said, looking down at him all dressed up in a black suit and white shirt. His lips were stretched tight, his front row of gold teeth showing because he had been proud of them.

When Annie came back to work after Rodney died, she was quiet. Mama didn't know what to say to her, and everybody moved around the house as if they were in a church or a funeral home. The only sound was the vacuum cleaner when Annie turned it on. That day she vacuumed and vacuumed, every room in the house. I stood around the corner and watched as Annie vacuumed the same place over and over, sweating hard, breathing hard, and vacuuming as if she were killing snakes.

"She won't talk, and I don't know what to say to her," I heard Mama say to Sallie's mother on the telephone.

§

When I won Teacher of the Year for my school, Annie was losing her eyesight and her hearing. Mama told me that Annie couldn't see how to dust anymore and that she missed whole patches with the vacuum cleaner. "I'm keeping her on because I hate to let her go," she told me.

"I wish her daddy was here to see this," Mama said to Annie as the two of them rocked together on the back porch, the sun filtering through the pecan trees and making light and dark patches on the grass. "He would be swelled up with pride."

"He know it," said Annie. "The dead knows and looks after us from over yonder."

"I'm not so sure," said Mama. "If they can see the good, they can also see the bad, and then Heaven wouldn't be Heaven. They'd have to worry, and I don't believe there's any worrying in Heaven."

"They knows everything," said Annie. "They knows the whole story."

§

The day before my mother died, long after Annie had gotten too old to work any more, Mama sat in her wheelchair, her body swelled with the fluid that came from ovarian cancer, her eyes closed and her arms too weak to lift. She began whispering something, and I leaned close to hear. "Poor Annie," she said.

"Mama, do you want me to call Annie?" I asked.

Mama was too weak to speak above a whisper, but she nodded her head slowly.

"She can't talk," said the child who answered the phone. "She can't hear."

"Tell Annie that Mama is real sick," I said. "She may not be here much longer."

When the doorbell rang, Annie stood on the stoop, a rag tied around her bald head and wearing bedroom shoes and a frayed blue housecoat. She was a tiny brown thing who stood on her tiptoes and put her arms around me as I sobbed on her thin shoulders. Standing beside her was a teenaged boy who had driven her there.

Annie came inside and shuffled into the family room where Mama sat in the blue Lazy Boy recliner she died in the next day, her arms by her side. Suddenly, both her arms went straight into the air for the first time all day, and Annie fell onto her. Someone brought up a chair, and Annie sat beside Mama for a long time, their fingers intertwined like two lovers never wanting to let go. When Annie began to leave, Mama raised her arm again and pointed to her cheek where Annie leaned over and gave her one of her big sloppy kisses. When I thanked Annie for coming, all she said was, "That yo' Mama."

§

A week later, I went to see Annie. I drove to the projects and found the green trailer where Annie then lived with her son. I climbed the wobbly concrete block steps and knocked on the door. A voice called "come in," and I pulled open the metal door and stepped inside. Several children were chasing one another around the corners of the hot room, and a teenage boy lounged on the sofa, not looking up.

"I came to see Annie," I said.

"In there," the boy said, pointing to a side room.

I stepped into an immaculate room where Annie sat in a chair beside a bed, neatly made, the chenille bedspread the same length all the way around. I had brought her a white sweater that was Mama's with pink embroidered roses around the neck, a red Bundt pan, a nice set of knives, and a quilt for her bed. I sat on Annie's bed and faced her. Flies were walking along the shelves behind her head. I gave her the box containing the things I had brought her.

She touched each piece, and then she looked up and said, "You know what I really wants? I wants your Mama vacuum cleaner. I could run it up under my bed and get the dust kitties out. That's what I really wants."

I didn't know what to say. Suddenly that old vacuum cleaner became tinged with sentiment, and I couldn't bring myself to let it go. I knew that made me a terrible, mean, selfish person, but as soon as she asked for it, that old Electrolux loomed large with meaning in my mind, and giving it away would have been to give away my mother.

§

"She starts to hollering if she knows you," the young black female attendant said when I entered the nursing home to see Annie. "She can't see nor hear." When I took Annie's hand, she didn't know who I was. She couldn't tell if my hand was black or white. And she never started hollering.

At home, I slid the Electrolux box out of the closet and took out the blue fabric-covered hose with the chrome nozzle end. I fit the round brush end over the nozzle and coiled the whole thing down into a plastic Kroger sack.

When I went back to the nursing home, Annie was sitting in a wheelchair beside her bed. I pulled up a chair and sat down in front of her. Reaching into the grocery sack, I pulled out the hose with the brush end and put it into Annie's palm. I curved her fingers over the cold metal. Annie began to breathe heavily and then to holler loudly. I leaned in close and shouted into Annie's ear, "This is who I am!"

§

In her shiny silver casket Annie wore a pink lace dress with a high ruffle up under her chin, long puffy sleeves with cuffs around her wrists, and pink rhinestone earrings. Her cheeks were rouged, and her full lips painted red. On her head was a black wig with smooth straight bangs that lay across her brown forehead. She looked like a real lady and not like anybody's maid. When I said, "Yes Ma'am" out loud, the funeral director appeared in the doorway, a confused look on his face, as if he wasn't sure which of us had spoken.

"Patterns"

PATTERNS

"The pleasure lies not in the cookies, but in the pattern the crumbs make when the cookies crumble."

--Michael Korda

These are unceremoniously my new story beginnings:

One.

The only memorable event the entire evening was the bumblebee ring the couple said they had purchased as a fluke. She asked the question again and again: Don't you think it's the gaudiest thing you have ever seen? Don't you honestly? Honestly?

Two.

It is summer. For the first time, I am cleaning out my closets. I am deciding where to put this and that. I am discarding what I have no place for. I am building new shelves where none were before.

Three.

He tried to take it away from me. He dangled it in front of my face until I hated him with all my heart.

Four.

My life depends on mailing off stories and waiting peacefully in a chair until they come back, until at my door the shadow of the mailman hovers soundlessly, a silhouette in the afternoon sun.

Five.

This morning while reading an essay entitled "Post Hoc Fallacy," I learned that a rooster strutting from the barn each morning prior to the rising of the sun does not necessarily mean that the rooster causes the dawn.

Six.

I want my old job back and the peaceful relief of trail mix in bags already weighed and priced by the boys in produce. I want the items pre-arranged so I can take them in my hand and slide them past like a blessing. I can cup my hand over three small cans easy: one by one, three for a dollar.

II.

These are my new story middles, devoid of fanfare, inside and out, the real and true blood and guts and bones of it all:

One.

Bumblebees are not gaudy when buried, diazenon dead, in a pink althea bloom in spring. They are gaudy when, Midas gold on a long thin finger, they dig into the man's naval beneath his plaid cotton shirt. Far away from diazenon, gold-plated, studded with garnets, bumblebees smile dangerously deader than you, than I.

Two.

I am discarding old friends. I line my family members on shelves side by side in order, oldest to youngest. I hold this and that in the palm of my hand and turn my head from side to side. Shall I keep you, or shall I not? You wink at me as your breath turns sweet, and you die.

Three.

It is mine. It is the center of me. I will not give it to you no matter how hard you try, no matter how hard you cry.

Four.

The chair rocks across the floor with a rhythm only God can measure. The comfort of waiting is akin to hope and as far from despair as I from the inside of a green seedless grape.

Five.

Can I look behind to see why I am here and, in my looking,

discover where I will go next?

Six.

Peace is a tangible thing I can hold in my hand. It is a smooth shiny avocado, so ripe the skin is soft. Inside, given more space than necessary, the seed rattles.

III.

These are the endings of my new stories, without pomp and circumstance:

One.

In the end he doubles over. His head hits the floor kerplunk and the bumblebee ring is all she has left to remember him by.

Two.

At night the new shelves I built are so full they creak. Behind closed doors my family and friends whisper to one another in the dark.

Three.

I keep it still, wrapped in tissue in a blue velvet box in a special corner. Where is a secret.

Four.

In the living room a chair rocks slowly to a stop. In the quiet, the letters sound like pecans falling.

Five.

My roof is a stained-glass window. From here, I can see the springing bottoms of birds' three-toed feet.

Six.

The peace I have rolled in a brown grocery sack rattles as I walk. The first step is the farthest thing from my mind.

Acknowledgments

With appreciation to the following journals for publishing my stories: *Carolina Quarterly, Midway Journal, Chattahoochee Review, Los Angeles Review, Memphis Magazine, Gemini Magazine, Western Humanities Review,* and *Ascent.*

I would like to thank my family, Linda and Tom Waller, and the many cousins on both the Worsham and Fordham sides for loving and supporting me. Thank you also to Letha's sisters and brother-in-law for welcoming me into the family.

Thank you to my writing teachers: Sarah Gordon, Jill McCorkle, Alice Mattison, Sheila Kohler, Betsy Cox, Peter Selgin, and Allen Gee. Each of you brought something different to my work, and together, you helped me to find my own voice.

Thank you to Robert Canipe at Third Lung Press for believing in my book enough to want to see it published. You are a wonderful friend and a joy to work with.

Finally, thank you to Letha for your beautiful cover and inside illustrations. I love sitting beside you while you draw. Thank you also for your constant encouragement to keep writing. Thank you for believing in my ability and for the joy you bring to my life. I look forward to growing old with you.

§

Bio

Sandra Worsham's stories have been published in *Memphis Magazine*, *Carolina Quarterly*, *Western Humanities Review*, *Ascent*, and *Chattahoochee Review*, among others. She won First in Fiction in the Red Hen Press competition, and her story "Pinnacle" was published in the 2008 *Los Angeles Review*. Two of her stories were Finalists at *Glimmer Train*. After she retired from teaching writing to high school students for thirty years, her book on teaching writing, *Essential Ingredients: Recipes for Teaching Writing*, was published by ASCD in 2001. In 2017, her memoir, *Going to Wings*, was published by Third Lung Press. She was Georgia's 1982 Teacher of the Year and a 1992 Milken Award Winner. In 2000, she was inducted into the National Teachers Hall of Fame. In June, 2006, she received her MFA in Fiction from Bennington College. She lives in Milledgeville, Georgia, with her wife Letha and their two dogs.

§

Also Avaliable from Third Lung Press

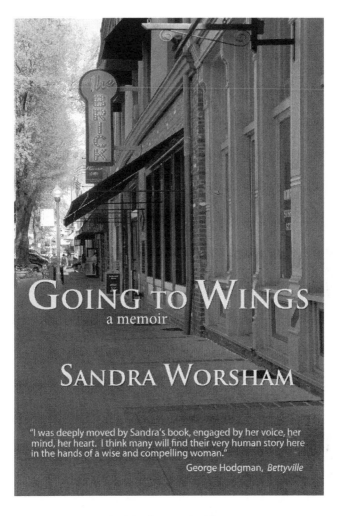

Also Avaliable from Third Lung Press

We Might as Well Eat

How to Survive Tornadoes, Alabama Football, and Your Southern Family

Terry Barr

Also Avaliable from Third Lung Press

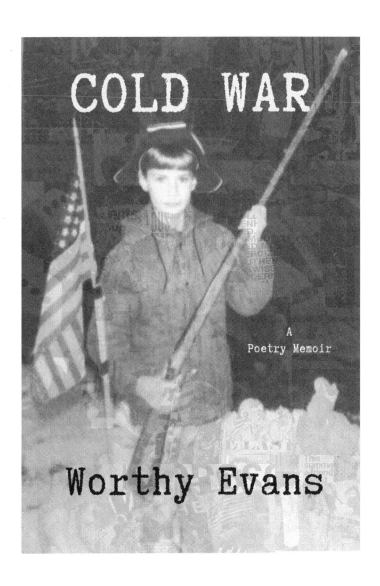

Also Avaliable from Third Lung Press

Made in the USA
Columbia, SC
26 June 2018